In Control

On a Wing and a Prayer

In Control
On a Wing and a Prayer

Priscilla Russell

Copyright © by Priscilla Russell

This is a work of inspired non-fiction. While most of the book content is true, names and identifying details have been changed to protect the privacy of everyone involved.

Unless otherwise noted, all materials on these pages are copywritten by Priscilla Russell. All rights reserved. No part of these pages, either text or image may be used for any purpose other than personal use. Therefore, reproduction, modification or retransmission in any form or by any means, for reasons other than personal use, is strictly prohibited without prior written permission.

Scripture references can be found at

https://www.biblegateway.com/

Cover Design and Interior Formatting

Allison Denise of BrandItBeautifully.com

Photography

Caylee Powell

Manuscript Editing

Tamika Sims of InkPenDiva.com

ISBN: 978-0-578-44252-5

ACKNOWLEDGEMENTS

I give all praise, honor, and thanks to our Lord and Savior Jesus Christ for His sustaining grace and mercy. Without it, I would have fallen by the wayside and forever lost. It was He who woke me up in the middle of the night with this vision and it was my God who made it possible. To my Mother, Queen Crenshaw who has never given up on any of her children, to God be the glory. She is the nucleus of my family, a true woman of God and a praying mother. Thank you for showing me how to love unconditionally and how to be a strong, yet nurturing woman. I love you. Special thanks to my nieces Latoya Moreland and Khadidr Jones for their late night and/or early morning proofing of this work. May God bless and prosper you both. To my family, I love each and every one of you. My prayer is that God will enlarge your territory and bless you indeed. To my Federal Aviation Administration family and friends, thank you for an awesome journey and wonderful career. It is the people that make the workplace special and Atlanta Center was nothing short of that. To the readers of this book, I hope it doesn't disappoint you; thank you for your support. To my step children; thank you for allowing me to be apart of your life. I love y'all. Last, but certainly not least, I want to thank my husband Billy Russell and son Devin Russell for their patience, support, understanding and the unwavering love they have given me throughout this process. I love you both, "more."

CONTENTS

PROLOGUE.. 1

CHAPTER ONE THE FORMATIVE YEARS.. 9

CHAPTER TWO WHAT IS AIR TRAFFIC CONTROL?............................. 23

CHAPTER THREE THE OLD COLLEGE TRY IS OUR CURSE 33

CHAPTER FOUR ONE LAST TRY.. 47

CHAPTER FIVE CROSSROADS.. 59

CHAPTER SIX THE EVOLUTION OF PATRICIA 73

CHAPTER SEVEN THE JOURNEY BEGINS... 101

CHAPTER EIGHT AIR TRAFFIC CONTROL: A RUDE AWAKENING
.... 121

CHAPTER NINE YOU CAN DEPEND ON GOD AND ONLY GOD ... 137

CHAPTER TEN ONE PHASE DOWN: FOUR MORE TO GO................ 147

Prologue

I was raised in a tongue talking, feet stomping, hand clapping, sanctified, Apostolic Overcoming Holiness Church located in the, "Heart of Dixie" Birmingham, Alabama. People refer to them nowadays as Charismatic or Pentecostal. Back in the day, we were affectionately referred to as, "Holy Rollers," or simply, "Crazy." The church I attended was small both in the physical size of the building that housed us, as well as the congregation. The sanctuary couldn't have been more than 700 square feet, but in the eyes of a child it seemed larger than a coliseum. We had about 50 members on roster and about half would show up on Sundays, most of which were families. There were the Walkers which included Sister Walker, her husband, who stopped coming to church after they were married, and her six children. Mr. Walker was the kind to find Christ, swear he's saved, then backslide the Sunday after the honeymoon. Then there was Sister Bateman and her tribe of five. I never knew what happened to her husband. As a kid, I thought she probably ate him. She was the meanest Saint I had ever seen. And then there was Pastor & Mrs. Lilburn and their family of six kids. Last, but certainly not least the Kershaws, that's us. There was my Dad who I do not remember ever setting foot in a church, (not even to be buried), my Mom a true saint, and a small pack of nine. We looked like a rainbow tribe. We came in all shades, sizes and colors. There were my six siblings and my two first cousins, (a boy and a girl) being raised by my mother. Oh, I can't forget my Grandmother, Mudear. I think that's slang for, "Mother Dear." Needless to say, my family was the largest in the small congregation and I was very aware of that fact. Not to mention, we were the better looking family, that is — other than the Pastor's family, but they didn't count. Did I mention that my Mom could blow? She could sing like an angel. She was, or shall I say is, very talented. Coconut brown with Egyptian features, she was exquisite and her name Queen said it all. Even the long dresses and lack of makeup or jewelry could not hide her beauty. My dad, Stan Senior, was a light, caramel colored, slender good-looking man. He was a sharp dresser and liked to drive nice cars. He always kept them clean. He didn't go to church and he was a real hell raiser. He was a complicated man whom I loved, feared, and hated simultaneously.

My two sisters were brick houses. The eldest Brenda was light complexion with thick, long, wavy, jet-black hair. She was a showstopper with much attitude. The middle girl, Janice, was light brown—the color of a smooth Hershey's chocolate bar. She once was on a plane with a famous singer and I swear she got more stares than the recording artist. She had pretty dimples, white teeth, and long, thick black hair with the prettiest slanted eyes you ever wanted to see. She was beautiful with a personality to match. Me, I was the youngest girl, skinny, light skinned, big pop eyes, and often referred to as cute. I always thought that was a code word for ugly. So I grew up thinking, I was the ugly duckling. My cousin Carol was on the chubby side. She was tall, solid, and she could dress. With silky mahogany colored skin and thick kinky hair, she looked like an African Princess.

My oldest brother Billy was a tall, ebony black, fine hunk. He talked a lot of trash and the women loved him. Wayne was next in line. He was the weird one of the bunch growing up, but I got to give him his props. The boy was fine and smart to boot. He was the brains in the family. His skin was the color of caramel. He had sexy eyes, pretty dimples, a nice physique with hair like cotton. He was also the meanest. No one messed with Wayne. Next in line was Earl. Earl was cool all his life. Even at the age of five, you could tell he was going to be the man. Almond brown with a slim built frame, he had big pretty brown eyes and a sexy smile. He was the quiet one, except when it came to the ladies. My other cousin, being raised by my Mom, was named Jason. He was tall, slim, dark, and handsome. He was a hustler. The ladies loved him, the men despised him, but nobody messed with him.

Now most of us could carry a tune, I guess we got that talent from my mom, but my baby brother Stan that boy is, "gifted" — just blessed. He's fine, grew up to be six feet tall, slender, pretty wavy hair, sexy dark brown eyes, and he has that smooth Native American bronze like complexion and features from my father's side of the family. He plays several instruments and the boy can sing. Anyway that's another book — back to this one.

Where was I? Oh yeah, we were raised in the Holiness church. Most of my friends were in the Holiness or Pentecostal Church as well. However unlike my Mom, their parents made them accept

Christ at an early age; whether they wanted to or not. Whether they believed or understood; it didn't seem to matter to them. But not my Mom, she gave us a choice. I didn't know why at the time, but now I understand that it's what God does to His children. I'm not saying she let us do what we wanted when we wanted; not at all. As kids, we were in church at minimum three days a week and all day Sunday. There was Tuesday night Bible Study, Thursday night mid- week service, Saturday some kind of fundraiser will happen, and choir rehearsal and then there was Sunday. Sundays were indeed full. She had to get as much God in us as possible because she knew He wouldn't see or hear from her kids again until Tuesday. So, there was early morning Sunday school, mid morning Sunday 11:00 am worship service, late afternoon Sunday Fellowship program, (at least twice a month), and Sunday night, "set the woods on fire," service. If our home church was not having a program, we were invited to one of our sister church's programs. On those Sundays, we would eat dinner at the church. Once Mom felt we were old enough to understand right from wrong, (usually around age 16 for her), and we had been given the proper foundation; she let us decide, "Whom we would serve?" And like most of my siblings, I took the long way around to get back to my beginnings.

I have always known I was special or predestined for some sort of greatness. I just didn't know for what until now. I wrote a paper in college once describing my birth as a miracle, because I couldn't wait to make it to the delivery room. I was born in the elevator. I think I used the word anxious. So, I was this miracle child of seven, who was neither the prettiest nor the smartest, but yet I was predestined....

CHAPTER ONE

THE FORMATIVE YEARS

It was July 30, 1963. The Civil Rights Movement was in full swing and I was born in the segregated South. Even at that young age, I was determined to make my mark, and do things a little different. On my way down to the, "Negro," floor of the University Hospital in Birmingham, Alabama, I decided to make my stand against discrimination and pop out on the elevator in-between the white floors. I guess you could say I was anxious to see what all the fuss was about. I mean with all the protesting, dogs, fire hoses, sit-ins and a man they called, "Bull Connor," things were crazy then in the South. Our President at the time was John F. Kennedy, Jr. Less than a month after I was born, on August 28, 1963, there was a big march on the capital led by Martin Luther

King, Jr. The march was for basic human rights and equality for Blacks, (or Negroes as they were called back then), in the United States. President Kennedy supported the march as well as the Civil Rights Movement. These two men were changing our Nation's history. Perhaps too fast for some, because before I would reach four months of age, President Kennedy would be dead and prior to my fifth birthday King would be assassinated.

I don't recall much of my early childhood. Just bits and pieces of things that may have shaped the person I am now. For example, I remember having my name changed in the first grade. I enrolled in school as a Moon, which was my mom's maiden name, but mid-way through I became a Kershaw. Everybody wanted to know if my mom got married or if I was adopted. I said no— I just have the same name as my dad now; that's all. I later learned that I was born out of wedlock. However, my dad must have really loved my mom and me because he married her.

You see he didn't just marry her, but he said I do to her four other children, a niece, a nephew, and her mother.

Another memory that sticks out in my mind is when I befriended a physically challenged girl in order to keep the boys from putting their hands up my dress. Thinking back, I find it hard to wrap my head around being sexually harassed as a third grader in elementary school. Where were the damn teachers? Perhaps, at a table by the building talking to each other or behind the building trying to sneak in a smoke. Who knows? What I do know is they were not paying us any attention. Besides, everyone knew the kids play time outside was a much-needed automatic break for teachers and they did not want to be disturbed. I didn't know what sexual harassment was, but even at the tender age of eight, I knew I didn't like it. I noticed the boys did not harass Sarah who had one hand smaller than the other. Therefore, being the natural survivor that I was or am; and wanting them to stop, I joined the ranks of the physically challenged and special kids to keep from being sexually harassed. It worked. It was as if their area had a force field around it. It was a safe zone and apparently off limits for what my mom called, "manish" boys. I often wondered why, but I'll keep my speculations to myself for now. I can't imagine what it's like on the playgrounds today.

I remember the first time I gave my life to Christ, I was almost 13. My mom started attending the headquarters church or the big church in Birmingham and they were having a revival. Every night they would have the unsaved come up, kneel at the altar, and tarry for the Holy Ghost. Tarrying for the Holy Ghost consisted of loud uptempo church music, saints or old folks standing over you shouting at the sinners to call on Jesus. I had been baptized by this time which was the main requirement for tarrying, so I was one of the sinners seeking the Holy Ghost. We would repeatedly call on the name of Jesus, until you foamed at the mouth, passed out from exhaustion or were overcome by the Holy Ghost and/or excitement and began to dance and speak in other tongues. It was the last night of the revival and I had left the altar unfilled again. I couldn't figure out what I was doing wrong. I really wanted the Holy Ghost. I wanted my mom to be proud of me. Sitting on my pew, the Bishop told us to stand and he began to pray. With my hands lifted and tears flowing down my face, I whispered here I am Lord; take me. I started calling on the name of Jesus as if my very life depended on it. The next thing I remembered was me getting up off the floor. I think I blacked out, but I couldn't remember. I remembered feeling confused. Was that the Holy Ghost? Had I been filled? Did anybody see me? Did I speak in tongues? All these questions raced through my mind but were never to be shared. Nonetheless, I stopped wearing pants for the rest of my 8th grade school year and tried to be on my best behavior in and out of school. To this day, I still don't know what I experienced; but it was something.

The last childhood memory I need to share is what I call the move. It was the summer after my third grade in elementary school, around May of 1972. I remember moving into this house that later became known as, "The Hill." It was the first house my parents owned. It was painted white with green shutters just like the ones we saw on television. It had an up and down stairs with a half basement. The half basement was not livable, but being the resourceful black family we were, that space with dirt walls became our storage room/storm shelter. With a family of 12, you waste nothing, not even space.

There were three bedrooms and a full bath upstairs. The largest bedroom had a walk-in closet. My mom gave that room to us four girls. It was the perfect size to hold the two queen sized beds we slept in. Oddly, I don't remember the color, but I remember its warmth and I remember feeling safe. Of course the boys were jealous and I'm sure my father was not very happy about the arrangement either. However, mom knew we needed the extra space.

The boy's bedroom was the second largest. Mom painted it a weird blue color. She said the color was supposed to relax you. It just made me sick. That tiny room had to sleep five. Being the creative, superwoman she was, she made it happen. She squeezed two sets of bunk beds and one hide away bed in that tiny space. The hide away bed was rolled out of a hall closet every night. To say it was really tight would be an understatement. Today, there are reality shows that glamourize and show you how to live in tiny houses or spaces. My mom was doing that in the 70s.

My parents had the smallest bedroom upstairs. It was a pinkish peach color that was fully furnished with a full size bedroom set. Her room was the only one upstairs that had dressers. Their room was at the top of the stairs and they could hear anybody coming or going.

Downstairs was the living room, a formal dining room which was converted to a bedroom for my grandmother, a den, a large kitchen, and a half bath. My mother bought all new furnishings for downstairs. This put my father in a lot of debt, which added additional stress to their already deteriorating relationship.

She had new shag carpeting, the color of gold, laid in the living room and den. The den had a multicolored couch and a floor model TV. It looked more like a big box of wood or a piece of furniture than a TV. The living room had a matching sofa, loveseat, and chair that were black and gold. The coffee and lamp tables were cherry wood with gold accents that matched the fabric of the couch. Back in the day, every middle class black family had a floor model stereo system in their living room, and we were no exception. The living room was spacious. It was so big my mom used the couch as a partition and voila she had her formal dining room back. She was determined to have a formal dining room. You see she had to, because all of the white family homes she cleaned as a young girl with her mother had one.

The dining room set was some sort of wood that had been painted an antique white. The top of the table, where you placed your plates, was a dark cherry wood. It was a beautiful piece of furniture. The table had six chairs with gold colored seat pads. Yeah, we all knew six chairs was not practical and down right ridiculous for 12 people. However, I believe my mom bought that set for show. It was like a showroom display set. A dining room set to be used by the grown ups. Besides, we only used it on holidays and special occasions. At which time we would gather additional chairs from all over the house for anybody who wanted to sit down at the grown folks table.

My mom converted the formal dining room into a bedroom for my Grandmother. Her room had a twin bedroom set that looked more like it belonged to little girls than a 60-year-old. I think my mom bought that set because it matched the downstairs décor. The twin beds had these high antebellum poles and the entire set was white with gold trimming.

I must say; my mom had that house looking like the ones in *Ebony* or *Jet* Magazine. The kids loved it. However, my dad was not thrilled about the mounting debt. He only worked at places that would pay him, "under the table," cash money. That often meant making less than regular folks. He was on disability and got a monthly check. He needed that check and three more for his large family. So the cash payments kept his disability check out of jeopardy. He got hurt while working in the coal mines of Alabama. I never knew how he got hurt or what his injury was, but lung cancer claimed him at 55.

Even with my mother working full time as a Licensed Practical Nurse, she had them in over their heads. My dad used to tell her, "You got more than any poe woman I know."

The house sat on a big hill. The front must have been two stories high. We had to cut the front yard with a rope tied to the lawn mower. We would literally tie a rope to the handle of the lawn mower and let it roll down the hill. The rope was used to pull it back up. It was too steep to push.

The backyard rolled downward. It had three levels with a walkway extending to the back door. That walkway created a right and left side for each level. On the first level, my mom bought a swing set and put it there across from the dog house. Our dog's name was Rex. He was a crazy dog with no training and extremely wild because he stayed chained up all the time. Nonetheless, whenever he felt like it, he would break loose and the entire neighborhood would run for their lives. "Rex loose," would echo through the streets and the kids would run for cover. Some kids would climb and hide in trees, others behind partitioned fences, and the ones that could make it home; hid out in their houses, and would not come back out until they knew it was safe. That included us. We were just as scared as the other kids. If you were too slow to get away; my brother would yell, "Freeze, don't move. Just stand still and let him sniff you." He really meant bite you. The only persons able to handle Rex were my grandmother, who was just as ornery as he was, and my middle brother Wayne. He would catch him and together they would chain him back up until the next break.

The second level had clothes lines on one side and the other side is where my grandmother planted a garden. There was an apple, a peach, a plum, and magnolia tree spread across this level.

The third level was an all cement patio. We put the lawn furniture out there, a barbeque grill, and once we even had an above ground swimming pool. The house was nice and although we did not know it at the time; it was considered a middle class mixed neighborhood. It was large and spacious compared to our last one. The walls were freshly painted which made the 17-year-old house seem new. We thought we were the black Brady Bunch baby and I was the black Cindy Brady in the flesh.

In less than 10 years, we had come from segregated everything in Birmingham, Alabama to a mixed neighborhood.

By the time I entered high school in the fall of 1977, we had experienced what was to become known, as the, "white flight," and our middle class mixed neighborhood had now become simply the hood. Back then hood was slang for working class black neighborhood.

CHAPTER TWO

WHAT IS AIR TRAFFIC CONTROL?

In May of 1981, I graduated from A. H. Parker High School. The President at the time was Ronald Reagan. On August 5, 1981, he gave an order that changed the landscape and faces of Air Traffic Control. This order would dismantle the, "good ole boy," system that had been ingrained in the Federal Aviation Administration (FAA) for decades and opened the door for true diversity in the administration. This order afforded women and people of color opportunities that would have otherwise not been available. That order altered the course of my life forever.

I vividly remember my mother sitting in our den watching the news. As I started to ask her if I could use her car to go to the store, which was code for go hang out and smoke a joint, she shushed me and said be quiet. It was then I heard the reporter stating that Reagan had fired over 11,000 air traffic controllers who refused to return to work.

The following is an excerpt from Wikipedia:

At 7 a.m. on August 3, 1981, the union declared a strike, seeking better working conditions, better pay, and a 32-hour workweek (a four-day week and a eight-hour day combined). In addition, PATCO wanted to be excluded from the civil service clauses that it had long disliked. In striking, the union violated 5 U.S.C. (Supp. III 1956) 118p (now 5 U.S.C. § 7311), which prohibits strikes by federal government employees. Ronald Reagan declared the PATCO strike a "peril to national safety" and ordered them back to work under the terms of the Taft-Hartley Act. Only 1,300 of the nearly 13,000 controllers returned to work.[5] Subsequently, at 10:55 a.m., Reagan *included the following in a statement to the media from the Rose Garden of the White House: "Let me read the solemn oath taken by each of these employees, a sworn affidavit, when they accepted their jobs: 'I am not participating in any strike against the Government of the United States or any agency thereof, and I will not so participate while an employee of the Government of the United States or any agency thereof.'"[7] He then demanded those remaining on strike return to work within 48 hours, otherwise their jobs would be forfeited. At the same time, Transportation Secretary, <u>Drew Lewis,</u> organized for replacements and started contingency plans. By prioritizing and cutting flights severely, and even adopting methods of air traffic management that PATCO had previously lobbied for, the government was initially able to have 50% of flights available.[5]*

On August 5, following the PATCO workers' refusal to return to work, Reagan fired the 11,345 *striking air traffic controllers who had ignored the order,[8][9] and banned them from federal service for life. In the wake of the strike and mass firings, the FAA was faced with the task of hiring and training enough controllers to replace those that had been fired, a hard problem to fix as, at the time, it took three years in normal conditions to train a new controller.[2] They were replaced initially with non-participating controllers, supervisors, staff personnel, some non-rated personnel, and in some cases by controllers transferred temporarily from other facilities. Some military controllers were also used until replacements could be trained. The FAA had initially claimed that staffing levels would be restored within two years; however, it would take closer to ten years before the overall staffing levels returned to normal.[2] PATCO was <u>decertified</u> by the <u>Federal Labor Relations Authority</u> on October 22, 1981.*

Back then, I didn't even know what an air traffic controller was or what they did, but I knew it had to be something special because they made the news. I now know that air traffic controllers are responsible for the safe, orderly and expeditious flow of air traffic, or as I tell my young nieces and nephews, we're the traffic cops for aircrafts. Many years later, after I became an air traffic controller, I found out the behind the scenes of that epic firing.

In 1981, the air traffic controllers had a strong and extremely powerful union that represented them. That union was the Professional Air Traffic Controllers Organization. It was affectionately known as PATCO. PATCO was formed in 1968; so you see, they had been around making demands for higher pay and better working conditions for a long time and had dealt with countless Presidents. They ran the FAA and treated would be controllers as if they were pledging a fraternity.

The union heads were convinced that President Reagan would not and could not fire all of them. So the controllers, who are Federal Employees, went on strike. It was and still is illegal for Federal Employees to strike against the Federal Government. When they refused President Reagan's order to return to work, he gave them their walking papers.

In the months to follow, the government along with the Federal Aviation Administration (FAA) scrambled to keep the National Airspace System (NAS) running. They had to find controllers to work the approach control option (at the airport) as well as the Air Route Control Center (ARTCC) options.

Here's a simpler breakdown of the two. Approach Controls in the 80s were located at the airports. They were called up and down facilities, because the controllers worked up stairs in the tower and downstairs on radar positions in the approach control room. The controllers in the tower are the ones that clear the planes to land and take off. They only control the aircraft they can physically see and when needed they would use binoculars to aid them. The tower control would hand off the aircraft to the controller downstairs working radar. This controller would work the aircraft in his or her airspace. This airspace was usually a small, defined radius around the airport not higher than 14,000 feet. As the aircraft flew higher and got further away from the airport, the approach control would hand the aircraft off to the ARTC Center. There were 20 centers throughout the country. The centers would work the aircraft across state lines and implement restrictions to slow down and spread out the aircraft.

The FAA had its work cut out for them. They had a lot of positions to fill and they needed them filled quickly. They ordered every staff person from their Regional Offices, from their headquarters in Washington, and from the local facilities back to the controller ranks to work traffic. It didn't matter if you had not talked to an aircraft in over 10 years, or if you felt confident in your abilities to control traffic. And it did not matter whether or not you were proficient. The bottom line was the FAA needed controllers and all those concerns were luxuries the Administration could not afford. They brought in controllers from the military to work the approach controls. They even brought back controllers who had recently retired. However, they soon realized it would not be enough. It became clear that the FAA Academy needed to be inundated with students. In addition, it became evident that the 5 to 7 years it took to train an individual to become a Full Performance Level (FPL) Controller had to be shortened.

The FAA developed an accelerated program that would enable a person to become an FPL in less than 2 ½ years at their busier and more complex facilities; and, less than 2 years at others.

They needed the brightest young minds they could find or special people with type A personalities. The Business Dictionary defines a Type A Personality as: A temperament characterized by excessive ambition, aggression, competitiveness, drive, impatience, need for control, focus on quantity over quality and unrealistic sense of urgency. It is commonly associated with risk of coronary disease and other stress-related ailments.

There was a massive off the street hiring, but the majority of the applicants could not pass the exam. Soon the FAA started to recruit at Universities and Colleges around the country. They were on almost every campus across America including the Historically Black Colleges and Universities (HBCUs). They needed controllers desperately; in fact, they needed them yesterday.

CHAPTER THREE

THE OLD COLLEGE TRY IS OUR CURSE

It was the Fall of 1981. My mind, body, and spirit were all changing along with the season. I was working part-time as a cashier in a grocery store. I was drinking as often as possible, getting high, and smoking up to a pack of cigarettes a day. I was an 18-year-old, grown ass woman; who just happened to be living with her mom. I was old enough to legally buy alcohol. I was old enough to be tried as an adult. I was even old enough to be drafted in the military and possibly die for my country. According to the law of the land, I was LE –GAL- LY grown; except in my Mama's house. Apparently, she didn't know about those laws. Besides, who was I to educate her? The rest of her children didn't. She did not play with children. The only laws observed in her house were found in the Bible. So, there was no alcohol, no tobacco, and definitely no marijuana being bought, consumed or ingested by anyone under her roof, (or at least that she knew about).

Mom didn't like the changes she was seeing in me. She tried to fix me, the only way she knew how, with more restrictions and house rules.

"You need to be home by midnight."

"You can't go out tonight."

"I don't want you hanging around with her."

Not to mention her constant nagging about going to school.

"You need to get in somebody's school; so you can get a good job."

"I know ma Okay already!"

I hated the new rules Mom had in place to fix me. I didn't like living at home and I was not feeling going to college. I had already been in school 13 out of the 18 years of my life. I truly believed it would be a waste of my time, because all of my older siblings had gone to college or trade school and none of them had finished.

My oldest brother, Billy, took mechanical drawing in high school. He was actually good at it. He wanted to be an Architect or a Mechanical Engineer. He enrolled at Mills College after graduation in pursuit of his degree. During his second year of college, he pledged one of the largest black fraternities in the nation. Afterwards, he did more partying than studying and eventually dropped out. Next off to college was my eldest sister Brenda. She was to follow in the footsteps of my Mom and become a Nurse. However, hanging in the student lounge playing cards got the best of her. My sister-cousin Carol went to cosmetology school. I'm not exactly sure what happened with that. All I know is that...it didn't happen. The next two Janice and Wayne made the mistake of going to the University of

Alabama in Birmingham. Let's just say the South still had some issues even in the early eighties. However, Wayne got his bachelor's degree after serving in the military many years later.

It was now my turn to give it the old college try. I didn't want to make the same mistakes as my siblings, who had all gone to college, but did not graduate. I was scared and unsure of myself. My sisters were beautiful; my brothers good looking. All of them were intelligent and talented. If they couldn't finish, I didn't stand a chance. Remember, I was the," cute one," (code for ugly duckling), and I wasn't as smart. It didn't matter how I felt. When my Mom said go, we went.

I enrolled in Livingston State Community College to become an X-Ray Technician. I picked that major because of Reginald; the guy I was dating at the time. He worked in the X-Ray Department at the University of Alabama Birmingham (UAB) Hospital. He drove a nice car so I figured they had to pay pretty decent. Besides how hard could it be?

I got off to a rocky start. The first year and a half after my high school graduation was a blur. The classes were extremely difficult. I didn't realize the tremendous amount of biology and science classes that were involved in the curriculum. I hated biology and science. My classes got increasingly harder along with the drugs I was taking. I needed to be more alert when I studied; cocaine was my drug of choice. It was just what the doctor ordered. I used cocaine to pick me up and weed with a shot of whatever brand of liquor I had to bring me down.

Even with that, I was still failing. I needed help. I needed a way out. I went to my counselor and she told me I could withdraw from the classes. She said I could take a "W" in place of the obvious "F" I was sure to receive. I would just have to retake the class before the "W" was converted to an "F." I didn't bother to ask how long I had before the conversion would occur, I just told her to do it.

After withdrawing from those classes, I enrolled in The University of Alabama Birmingham (UAB). They had an Allied Health Program designed to train students in specialized medical health fields in half the time it would normally take. That was perfect for me. I needed half the time, because I had already wasted a year at Livingston State Community College. I kept the same major of X-Ray Technology. I believed I had an advantage. I knew what to expect. For some reason, I thought the biology and science courses at UAB would be easier. They had to be because I had already gone through them at the Community College. They weren't. They didn't even have the same books.

My first class was held in a room the size of my high school auditorium. It had a gradual slope that led to the Professor's podium. There must have been over 200 students in the room. Even though I was the only black female, out of a handful of blacks, I felt invisible. It felt like waves hitting me; the sea of white faces turning my way. And though I held their gaze for a brief moment, it was as if none of them saw me; at least not the real me. While looking around for a seat, I heard my heart beating rapidly and my hands started to sweat. Thinking back, I'm not sure if I was experiencing a panic attack or if I needed a fix. Either way, I sat as close to an exit as possible; in the event a quick escape was needed.

The professor began his lecture on medical and radiological terminology. It was as if he was speaking in a foreign language. I needed this to be over quickly. Exactly one hour and two minutes into his lecture I started looking around. I thought to myself, did I miss the bell? Getting annoyed I looked at the clock again and confirmed he was now three minutes over. However, no one else in the class seemed to be concerned that this guy was going over his allotted time.

I was in need of my morning medication. I needed a cigarette and a bump of coke, (slang for sniff of cocaine), ASAP. I started looking around for my class schedule. I was relieved to find it crumpled up in the bottom of my purse. *Yes here it is.* I straightened the paper out as I thought to myself. *What day is it? I never take classes on Mondays. Can't make it on time after a weekend. Oh yeah, here it is. Tuesday, the first class is from 12pm till 3pm. Wait a minute. Is this right?*

"Three hours!"

The next thing I knew; I was having an out of body conversation, in my mind, with myself and it went something like this:

"Did I just say that out loud or am I still high?"

"You must have idiot. People are looking at you. The Professor is looking at you."

"Oh shit. You mean, I'm no longer invisible!"

Looking directly at me, he stopped speaking in that foreign language. I was finally able to understand every word he said.

"Yes this is a 3-hour lecture. We will have a brief 10 minute break soon."

At exactly 1 hour and 20 minutes into his lecture, the Professor gave us a break. Needless to say, I didn't go back to class.

I was going to have to drop out of school again. I could not believe it! How did I get here? Was there some type of curse on me? On my sisters and my brothers? As I pondered these thoughts, generational curses came to mind.

The Apostolic Overcoming Holiness (AOH) Church defined a Generational Curse as a spiritual bondage that is passed down from one generation to another.

Paula White on paulawhite.org explains it this way. **Iniquity** *is the practice of sin to the point it becomes pleasurable; or* **a predisposition to sin,**

which is a weakness to yield to that sin in particular and is passed from generation to generation. *In life, we will deal with recurrent situations, or patterns of behavior that cannot be explained solely in terms of what happened in your lifetime. Sometimes, the things you fall down to really have nothing to do with you, but are a predisposition you inherited from your ancestors who fell down easily to the same things!*

The first time I heard the term generational curse was during testimony services at our home church, The Greater Temple AOH Church of the Living God, Inc. Testimony service was a time set aside, during praise and worship, when folks seemed to tell all their business. Mom would make each of us testify. It didn't matter if it was good, bad, or indifferent; you had to say something.

I felt her nudge and realized it was my turn. I quickly stood to my feet and in my loudest church voice said, " I thank God for my life, health and strength." Members of the congregation echoed," Amen," "Amen," throughout the sanctuary. After my short and simple testimony, Sister Walker rose to her feet and said in her most sanctimonious voice," Praise the Lord saints!" The congregation responded, "Praise the Lord!" She then proceeded to tell the entire congregation that her lights were off, her car was not running, and she only had two dollars in her purse. She ended her testimony with, "Y'all pray my strength in the Lawd."

Testimonies like those were common. It seemed as if the closer you were to God, the harder your life got. All the saved-sanctified folks in my church were going through hell here on earth and I wanted no part of that. But I'll never forget the time Mother Parker told us, I mean testified, about her family's generational curses. She told us that her father had spent most of his life in prison; her two sons were inmates and her oldest grandson had been sentenced to life in prison for murder. She cried out, "Lawd, my God break these generational curses binding my family!"

It sent chills up my spine as I stared in confusion and then fear. Who would curse sweet Mother Parker? Was it somebody in the church? Was it that mean Mother Bateman? I hope she doesn't curse me.

My mom would sometimes testify about our family's generational curses. She had alcoholism passed down to her and her siblings from their parents. Both she, her two sisters, and their two brothers, were all alcoholics. Her oldest brother fell to his death out of an open window. The autopsy confirmed he was intoxicated. My Mom would tell the congregation how finding Christ saved their lives. My Mom, Grandmother and Uncle would be delivered from their generation.

However, it seemed as if an additional curse was added with every new generation. We had my Mom's generation to thank for getting pregnant out of wedlock. Me and my sisters, like my mother and her sisters would all have babies before we were married. My generation's curses could possibly be the worst of them all. My siblings and I would be adding to the list of curses: drug addiction and the inability to obtain a college degree.

By January of 1983 all, but two of my Mom's children had graduated from high school. None had finished college. Two of my brothers were strung out on drugs and another was an alcoholic. As for me, I was battling both addictions.

I remembered Mother Parker's testimony from when I was a young girl. I cried out loud just as she had," Lord help! My family needs You. Help me break these generational curses."

The following week my Mom sat me down and after a long talk, she said,

"You been out here running around for too long. You smarter than that. Why don't you go on out there to Mills College? I think that will be a better fit for you."

For the first time in years, I took my Mom's advice.

CHAPTER FOUR

ONE LAST TRY

When the fall of 1983 rolled around, I was a student at Mills College. Mills was a predominantly black college on the outskirts of Birmingham, Alabama, in a city called Midfield. The college was very small. We had two dorms, one for the girls and one for the boys. There was a row of about eight apartments for the upper graduates and young faculty members who had not yet found permanent housing. Both the dorms and apartments were in need of repairs, but for the most part they were clean. Apparently, the powers that be thought paint could fix anything. For example: air seeping through cracks in the window seals, slap some paint on it; door squeaks, slap some paint on it; heater broke, paint it and use it for a table.

The cafeteria and our student union center were in the same building. The cafeteria occupied the entire first floor of the building and the student union center encompassed the entire second level directly above it. The student union, which was actually one large room, had two Ping-Pong tables, a card table and a sitting area with a T.V. There were three offices located there; two for Academic Counselors and the other for the officers of the Student Union Body. The front of the building was all glass allowing you a completely un-obscured view of the immaculately manicured landscape. Beautiful flowers bloomed year-round adding color and excitement to the campus. Beautiful trees and walkways lined the small campus and connected the buildings like a picture-perfect puzzle. It was prettier outside than most of the places inside on campus. There were two small buildings that looked more like country churches than college buildings. One housed Business Majors and the other was home to History Majors. There was another building used for Music Majors which looked more like an old gymnasium. I think it was once used as a band room, but since we didn't have a choir building, we used it for the Symphony and Gospel Choir rehearsals. I was a member of the Gospel Choir. Next to the choir building was a small shotgun house used by the Drama Department, for the acting classes. The newest and only modern building on campus was the Communications Building. It had a lot of high-tech equipment used by the Communications Department. I loved being there. That building was my reason for majoring in Communications. The student library was there as well. Our Financial Aid building and Main Hall looked like a small elementary school that had been converted into many small offices. The front of the building had four large stone columns that looked as if they had been shipped from Rome. They made the campus look prestigious. This building was the focal point and first thing you saw as you approached the campus. The gymnasium was the only building located off campus; it was one block south of the back-entrance gate.

A gym class was required. Every student had to take at least one credit hour. I took a square-dancing class to meet my credit requirement. I thought, why not? An easy "A" right? Wrong. There were entirely too many styles of dances and way too many rules for me. I didn't like it very much. We would walk up to the gym, dance for an hour and then walk back to our other classes. I hated walking to my gym class. Even though I was in pretty good shape; I would still be exhausted afterwards. Needless to say, with all the rules and different dances the class was not an easy "A." After forgetting where to start and when to doe-si-doe; I barely swung out of there with a "B." That taught me to never assume that a class/course would be an easy push over, but be ready for whatever may come.

It was my sophomore year and I was standing in the hallway reading information on a bulletin board in front of the Student Placement Center (SPC). The SPC was where the smart students went to look for good jobs. This time around I was focused on school. I had a different commitment level and I was determined to graduate. Not to mention, I wanted/needed a good job. I didn't want to wind-up like most of the college graduates I knew; working as a Manager for some fast-food service or drug store chain. Black College graduates of the 80s didn't have it as good as the blacks who had graduated a decade earlier. The young college educated blacks of the 70s, who were still reaping the benefits of the Civil Rights Movement and Affirmative Action, were practically guaranteed a corporate or government job simply because they had a college degree. That was short lived. The young college educated blacks in the 80s were just looking to get a job that would pay above the minimum wage. However,

I don't think this was the case for the young educated whites.

While reading, I felt a tap on my shoulder and heard Maria saying, "Hey," to get my attention. Maria was my best friend on campus. She was a short brown-skinned sassy chick with hazel eyes. She was a beautiful girl. All the guys were crazy about her. She was cool and absolutely fun to be around; we had a lot in common. She got high and liked to party, just like me. She came from a large dysfunctional family, just like me. She had a part-time job, a determination to do better, an inner drive, and was slightly off; just like me.

I turned and Maria said, "Hey Trish, are you going to assembly today?"

Trish was my nickname. Every black person I knew had a nickname; including Maria and all my siblings. Nicknames like: June Bug, Pee Wee, Pokey, Cookie, Slim, Lil Bit, Red and Big Boy were common. And if you didn't have a nickname that fit you, folks just abbreviated your birth name.

"Hey Ria, what's up? I guess so, what else is there to do?"

"We could skip and go smoke this blunt or something."

"Not today Chick, it's my sophomore year and I've got to try to get an internship of some sort or its hello Uncle Sam for me. It says on the board that we're having a guest speaker from the F.A.A. here recruiting."

"The what?— What's the "F" whatever?"

"The F.A.A.— Well— let me see— it's the Federal Aviation Administration, whatever that is."

"Yeah well— okay Trish, I guess I'll come sit with you."

"Cool let's go, it starts in a few minutes."

The first half was as boring as ever. I found myself staring around the auditorium thinking of mostly nothing, when all of a sudden this voice of thunder caught my attention. It was, "The Man," Mr. Greg Darnet, the recruiter from the FAA. He was a tall, hazel colored, well-dressed man. It was clear he had been a heart-throb in his day. However, in the eyes of a 20-year-old, he was just another old man. He must have been in his mid to late fifties. He spoke very fluently and with confidence. He went on and on about things I didn't care about like, "What are you going to do with your life," and, "the contributions we're expected to make to society," and on and on. I thought I was going to scream. I was thinking, I should have taken Maria up on her offer to smoke that joint, when I heard Mr. Darnet say, "How would you like to make over $50,000 a year within two years after you graduate?" I didn't know how or what I had to do to make that kind of money, but I knew that was the job for me. Whoever said money was a motivator— knew what they were talking about. Fifty grand a year was a lot of money back then.

After the assembly I went to the Placement Center for information. I found out that the job was something called an Air Traffic Controller and I had to take a test to get hired. I wasn't exactly sure what they did, but I remembered President Reagan fired a lot of them in the summer of 1981. They probably needed a lot of help. I filled out the paperwork required by the FAA and the college to take the exam. Just my luck, the test would be the following Saturday. The test would last several hours with breaks between sections. They advised us we would spend most of the day there. I couldn't believe they would screw up a weekend like that, but the chance to make fifty grand was worth it.

I showed up for the test sleepy, tired and hungover. While taking the test I was thinking, I don't know what the big deal is and this doesn't seem too bad. Of course I finished early and proudly turned my test in to Mr. Darnet.

"I'm finished Mr. Darnet."

"I see. — Please wait one moment; while I look it over."

I thought to myself sure no problem I know everything is good. After what seemed like an eternity he looked me square in the eyes and said, "Young Lady, I can see, you do not take your career seriously." I stared him straight in his eyes. *Say what old man? You don't know my story. This is the first time in a long time I've been serious. What you trying to say?*

Mr. Darnet rudely interrupted my thoughts with his stupid question, "Is there anything else young lady?"

"Oh— no, thank you."

He gave me a head nod dismissal. I left angry and confused.

I called my girl Maria as soon as I got to the house.

"Hey Maria, you got time to talk?"

"Hey Trish. You called me by my real name. What's up?" I proceeded to tell her all about my day. I spared no detail.

"For real Ria, just who does he think he is and what exactly did he mean by that statement? I can see you do not take your career seriously." I take everything seriously—shit! That's why I showed up."

"Girl forget about him. He doesn't know what he's talking about. You wanna go to a party with me tonight?"

"Who's having a party?

"It's a Frat party on campus."

"Sure, why not. I need a release."

CHAPTER FIVE

CROSSROADS

Maria, picked me up early for the Frat party. We needed time to score without missing any of the excitement. We arrived at the Student Union Building and went upstairs to see if the party was jumping. It was slow so we decided to stroll the campus looking for some weed and a little blow. It didn't take long for us to find both. The Brickyard Housing Projects sat directly across the street. There were several dealers slinging out of the projects. The only thing separating the Brickyard Tenants from the Mills students was a narrow street and a row of evergreen shrubs with sections of a rusted chain link fence intertwined. Mills, like most HBCUs, was located in a low-income area. The Black Institutions weren't designed or built that way, it just happened over time. Most of the HBCUs were opened in the 1800s when the landscape was a lot different. There was probably nothing within a 15-mile radius of most of the schools when they were built. Their founding fathers did not know that neighborhoods would nearly swallow up their private oasis. And those neighborhoods would later become ghettos or hoods.

Oddly enough, crossing that narrow street onto the campus grounds felt as if you had traveled back in time. The campus looked nothing like the poverty stricken neighborhoods it was surrounded by. It had a way of making you forget your surroundings. Being on campus gave you a false sense of security that caused you to let your guard down.

Dave, a short, stocky and fairly muscular character was the dealer we copped our drugs from that night. He was standing in their usual spot, on the south corner of the parking area near the Student Union Building. After we purchased our goods Maria said, "We need a place to split this up." Neither of us stayed on campus. We both commuted to and from school daily. Dave said, "Y'all can come with me." He told us he was a friend of Mr. Morgan, one of our newest Faculty Members, and we could go to his place. Maria and I looked at each other, hunched our shoulders and said, "Okay." We just wanted to get high. Besides, Mr. Morgan's place was only a few feet away in the Faculty Apartments on campus.

Dave knocked loudly on the door. Mr. Morgan opened it without hesitation and without asking who we were. He must have been expecting him, because he didn't have a peephole and none of us had a cell phone. Cell phones in the 80s were big, bulky and expensive. I didn't know of anyone personally, not even a drug dealer who carried one. Most of them had beepers.

Mr. Morgan looked confused when he saw us. Dave said, "They cool man. Let us in, I got 'sum fo' you." Mr. Morgan, a medium height, skinny, dark brother with big pop eyes, reluctantly waved us in. Before he closed the door, he looked around outside to make sure no one had seen us entering his apartment. Although Mr. Morgan looked like he was in his mid to late forties, we later found out he was only eight years older than we were. It was evident that the drugs he abused, had abused him.

We entered a dimly lit living room. There was a couch, a chair, and two tables. One table held a lamp, which had a red light bulb in it. The other was a square coffee table. That's where Dave went to work like a chemistry student in a lab. He set out a big stash of cocaine and told us to put ours back. It was obvious, he wanted to impress us and we were more than happy to let him. Mr. Morgan started pulling out devices I had never seen before. Dave took the white powder, I had always snorted and sprinkled it in a big spoon. Next, he added another powder mixture and a few tiny drops of water. Then he took a cigarette lighter and placed the fire under the spoon. Dave looked at us and said, "This is how you cook this shit!" I looked around the room and observed Mr. Morgan. His eyes were fixated on the rocks that were being cooked. He was shaking. Perhaps from anticipation or maybe he simply needed a fix. All the while Dave was preparing the rocks, we were drinking, talking trash and smoking some fye ass weed.

After what seemed like an eternity, Dave took a rock and placed it on what looked like a glass pipe. He gave the pipe to Mr. Morgan. Mr. Morgan took a lighter, lit the small bubble end that housed the rock and inhaled. He sucked in again and again until the sound of cracking and popping stopped. Mr. Morgan gently placed the pipe on the table. Afterwards, he slumped back into the couch and drifted into a world far away.

Dave picked up the pipe, placed another rock on top and gave it to Maria. She lit, inhaled and relit until it was all gone.

This time Dave took the pipe, stood up, walked toward the back of the house while motioning for me to follow. My judgement was doubly impaired. I was high from that killer weed and I was on campus. Warning sirens were going off in my head as I thought, Where the hell is he going? Before I could process everything, my body started to move on its own, as if I were possessed. Someone or something was controlling my legs. I was following him into what looked like a bedroom without my sober consent. I entered the room and looked around. Shit, is this a damn bedroom? Okay, alright, it's still good. Surely, he won't try nothing crazy. Not on campus and not with my girl and ah what's his name up front.

Dave was speaking, but I only heard him say, "Come on back here girl ain't nobody 'gon hurt ya. Don't cha wanna hit this?" I instantly relaxed again as the drugs lulled me into a false sense of security. I thought, oh good, he must have been reading my mind. See there, he said he wasn't gon hurt me. Enjoy! The bedroom was even smaller than the living room with lowlights. A blue light bulb had been placed in the light fixture located in the ceiling directly above the bed. I stood there thinking, what's with these colored bulbs and why is it so damn dark in this place? The room had a full size bed with a small table stand next to it. Dave sat on the bed and placed the goods on the stand. He tapped an area on the bed next to him twice and said, "Come try this." I sat on the small bed as far away as I could trying not to offend him. I wanted to be close enough to reach the pipe, but not too close for him to try something foolish.

Dave gave me the pipe. I took it and placed it to my lips. He took out his lighter, moved closer and lit the pipe. I inhaled deep like I had seen Maria and Mr. Morgan do earlier. He told me to hold it in. I did as I was instructed and held my breath as long as I could before coughing out what was left of the smoke. I repeated that ritual until the rock vanished.

My mind became foggy. I could not believe this feeling. I felt like what I envisioned Heaven would feel like. I felt free. Free of worries and free from pain. I was having an outer body experience. I saw myself floating in the air; or did it just feel as if I were floating in the air. I felt so good; it scared me. I was frightened. I was literally scared straight.

It was the first time in my life, I felt as though I had sinned against God. I had been taught all my life in the Holiness Church that your body was the temple of God. You kept your temple clean from sin by not drinking, smoking, fornicating, cursing, talking back to your elders, wearing makeup or tight clothing, and going to the movies. It was entirely too many restrictions to follow and/or uphold, matter of fact; by the time I was 18, I came to the conclusion that living was a sin and God was too hard to please. So, I stopped trying.

Oddly enough, I didn't believe my sin was the act of defiling my body with the drugs, nicotine or alcohol. No— this sin reached far deeper; deep into the depths of my soul. My mind, body, and spirit had become conscious of unadulterated pleasure. My sin was enjoying— no loving the sensation I was experiencing.

I realized something important that night. I discovered; when you're born and raised in a Holiness Church of, "The Living God," there are things you can't shake off. Teachings rooted deep inside of you that you don't realize are still there. Thoughts raced through my mind: Wow, this is crazy. I don't think I'm supposed to feel this good on earth. You can't serve two masters. Whoa— What is this? Did I die and go to Heaven? No other Gods before me. This is scary. I don't wanna ever feel this good, unless I've died and gone to Heaven. That was the first and last time I ever touched crack cocaine.

While I was having my out of body, back to Jesus, psychotic episode, Dave had been making his move. He was caressing my breast while kissing my cheek and neck. I came out of that trance with an automatic reflex. I pushed him back and yelled, "Stop! What the hell you doing?" He pushed me back and pinned me down with his body. I tried to break free, but the more I wiggled, the more turned on he seemed to become. I started crying, pleading, "Please don't. I'll pay you for the dope. I won't tell nobody." He lifted his body slightly to look at me. At first, I thought I saw confusion in his face. He was looking at me as if I had I lost my mind. But then I recognized the look. His frown was not one of confusion, but malice. That look awakened every defense mechanism inside of me and I went psycho. I was thinking, this nigga is the Devil! The Devil is after me and this nigga is trying to kill me.

He leaned in for a kiss and this time instead of turning my head. I clamped down on his bottom lip like a pitbull. I tried to bite it off. It caught him by surprise. When he pulled back to punch me, he loosened his grip. My adrenaline quickly took over and I turned into 'she-man.' My fear turned into rage. I started kicking and punching and screaming, "You gone have to kill me tonight. One of us gone die Nigga." It felt as if I was in a battle against Satan himself for my life. I had to win. He started yelling saying stuff I couldn't understand.

We fought until he got tired. Huffing and puffing he stopped, looked at me and said, "I'm tired. This shit ain't worth it."

Trembling, I got up and hurried to the living room. What the hell was Maria doing? Didn't she hear me screaming? The room was empty. They were gone. I did my best to pull it together. I fixed my clothes, ran my hands through my hair and walked towards the student union building. Maria was standing outside smoking a cigarette. As I approached her smiling face she said, "Hey chick you ready to par..." She stopped speaking mid sentence. Her smiling face had turned to one of concern and fear. The spot lights from the building had made me fully visible to her. She fired a series of short questions: "What's wrong? What happened? You okay? Did that nigga touch you?" I parted my lips to speak, but no words came out of my mouth. Words had been replaced by unintelligible sounds. I started to stutter as my breathing increased. I felt my eyes stretching; getting wider with each breath. I was hyperventilating. My heart was beating rapidly. I felt wet. I was confused and scared. What's happening to me? Am I having a panic attack? Maria grabbed me. Held me tight in her grip. We both sank to the ground. There she rocked me until it was over.

I was finally able to tell her what happened. She wanted to go to the campus security, but I just wanted to go home. Besides, what was I going to say? While breaking the law and campus rules of buying and consuming illegal narcotics, I was attacked. I couldn't risk getting kicked out of school. No, I had to stop crying, suck it up and keep it moving. Looking at Maria I said, "Just take me home please." There were no words spoken on that 20 minute drive home. None were needed. Her firm tender grip on my hand said it all. She loved me and would be there for me.

The next day I woke up stiff and sore. I struggled out of bed, walked over to the standing mirror in my bedroom, and examined my bruised body. Tears started to fall without my consent. I had promised myself I wouldn't cry about this again. Look at yourself. I turned from left to right. It looked as if I had been in a boxing match with Mike Tyson. I wiped my tears. I told myself it was over; I needed to be strong, but the tears kept falling. Damn!— What are you doing?— What is your purpose? Do you want to live or die? If you stay on this road, you gone end up in the ground.

I stayed in bed for three days. I told my Mom I had a stomach virus. She went on a 30 minute tirade saying things like: it was probably something I ate. I didn't wear enough clothes. I needed to stay out of the streets. I wasn't getting proper rest and I need to take better care of myself. I thought to myself, if you only knew. She's right. Some things gotta change. I was determined not to let this event break me. In fact, it had the complete opposite effect on me. I realized that night that I deserved better. I realized I was better.

Several weeks later, I received a letter from the FAA. After reading the letter, I found out what Mr. Darnet meant by his comment of me not taking my career seriously. He knew at a glance, I had failed their standardized hiring test. I was disappointed and embarrassed. After I stopped feeling sorry for myself, I decided to try again. *Didn't he say something about coming back? He'll see. Next time I'll be ready.*

CHAPTER SIX

THE EVOLUTION OF PATRICIA

It was summer time, school was out and it was hot in the dirty South. I needed another job. A friend told me that they were hiring at a new nightclub downtown called MR. V's. I figured why not, I had already worked at Burger King twice, Mcdonald's, The Merry-Go-Round, a phone solicitation company in which I do not remember the name, an electronic store, and a host of other part-time gigs that are too many to name. That summer as I waited to retake the test; I also waited tables at one of the hottest night clubs in town.

Around two thirty in the morning, after the club closed, my co-workers and I would make our way to an after hour joint. We took the tips we made and spent them on food, drinks and leaving big tips for the waiters. We had to let them know we were big tippers and were making big bucks; even if we weren't. Occasionally we would get some blow and then the party was really on. It was another wild and crazy summer. By the time it was over, I had increased my consumption of alcohol and cigarettes. But I had reduced my cocaine usage tremendously and I had completely stopped smoking weed. I never really liked the paranoid feeling it gave me.

The summer was winding down; the days were cooling off and I decided I needed to also. School would be in soon. I needed to get my head back in the game, settle down and refocus. But I had to get out of that night club, I needed a new part-time job. Working late nights would not be conducive to learning in early morning classes. I was fortunate to get my job back at the grocery store as a cashier.

The fall semester of 1984 had begun. The campus had come alive with young people from all walks of life. Freshmen orientation had wrapped up and most of them were still trying to get acclimated to their new home away from home; the upperclassmen who lived on campus were getting settled into their dorms; and we were all anxious to get registered for classes. But I needed money.

While most students were registering for their classes, I was in the Financial Aid Office trying to get my financial aid straight. That was an issue for me every semester. They never had my paperwork in order, despite the fact that I always turned it in before the deadline with everything completed. Maria, who had already registered, came along because she had nothing better to do. After waiting in line for 20 minutes, she came over and asked what was going on? I said, "It shouldn't be much longer. I never have anything left out of my Pell Grant after tuition and books? Hell, I get a loan every year and I still don't get crap back. What about you?"

"Look girl, I'm gone get what's mine. You just need to know how to work the system and lie if you have to."

"What are you talking about? — How do you lie?" At this point, she was looking at me as if I were special.

"Yes! — Lie. — You know. — On the information. — On the grant application." She was doing that pause speaking thing folks do when they think you're slow or don't quite get it.

"Oh — Okay, I see. Nah, my mom fills that out and she won't go for that. I guess I'll just be broke and hungry for the rest of my college days."

We laughed and talked until my name was called. I was able to secure finances and register for classes.

I had a new outlook on the way I approached school. I was a full-time student with a new found determination. I took as many hours as humanly possible for someone with a part-time job. I even took Saturday classes. I needed to make up for lost time. Six days a week my routine was as follows: a long early bus ride to school, go to classes, go to school library to research and study, a short bus ride to work, check out groceries 4 to 5 hours, a long bus ride home, do school work, wash dishes when needed, pass out in bed. Needless to say, that fall semester flew by. Before I knew it, the Spring Semester had begun.

Signs were posted all over campus with information about the FAA's Cooperative Education (CO-OP) Program. Mr. Darnet was scheduled to return to administer the hiring test after spring break. I immediately signed up. That night, after getting in from work, I called Maria. She picked up on the third ring.

"Hello."

"Hey Ria, have you heard?"

"Heard what?"

"That the FAA is coming back baby! After Spring Break, which is perfect! It'll give me time to study and prepare for Mr. Darnet."

"Mr. Darnet? What the hell he got to do with it?"

"You know he called me dumb last time."

"No he did not." Maria said matter of factly. "He said you weren't ready or something and you weren't then."

"He said serious." I corrected Maria in an annoyed voice. "Well— anyway, I need to prove him wrong! All I need is someone who is good in math to tutor me."

"Girl stop tripping, just ask your nerdy brother Wayne."

"You know for once, you're actually making sense. He is a Math and History major at UAB; if he can't help me no one can."

Wayne was a little different. He was somewhat temperamental. I had to approach him when he was in a good mood. Unfortunately for me, Wayne was seldom in a good mood. So, I just went for it.

"Come on Wayne I need your help. You're the only person I know who's good with numbers. The test has a lot of math on it and I need someone to explain it to me." I could see I had piqued his interest when I mentioned math.

"I'm not sure if I'll have the time. Shit, what type of math you talkin bout?"

"I'm glad you asked, here's a study guide I got from the library. This will give you an idea of what to expect on the test. Please—

pretty please Wayne."

"Yeah, Yeah, Alright. Yo got damn ass better do everything I say and the first time you don't show-up— well— hell that's it. That's gone be the end of free tutoring for yo dumbass."

Damn you such a grump. It don't make no sense for a young dude to be this mean. With a smile on my face I said, "Okay, I understand, thanks Wayne." I turned around and mumbled, "Crazy ass."

"What the hell you said?"

Oh shit, he heard me. "I didn't say nothing, damn!"

"I know you didn't!"

I turned and left with a sigh.

We studied for several weeks prior to the test. Those were the longest and toughest weeks of my life, up to that point. I had my big brother Wayne the grump as a professor and I couldn't withdraw from his class. He drilled me relentlessly.

"Alright listen dummy; if a plane leaves point A traveling at 480 knots?"

"Wait a minute what's knots again?" I asked trying not to sound too lost.

"I told you, think of it as miles an hour, shit!" He was clearly annoyed and I was getting tired of his abuse. This was my daily evening routine for over three long weeks. Me asking, "dumb" questions and Wayne yelling at me. Mom would give us her smile of approval when she left the house to pull her 4 to midnight shift at the hospital. That small gesture of encouragement made me want to work hard and not give up. So I stuck in there. I had to for Mom and it was worth it.

I showed up prepared to take the test this time. I took my time and was able to solve complicated abstract word problems. If I was not sure about one, I did what Wayne told me and picked, "C." But I didn't have to revert to that often. He had done an excellent job tutoring me.

After completing my test, I took a deep breath, gathered my things and approached Mr. Darnet. He was looking down reviewing the last test he had received. "Excuse me. Hello, Mr. Darnet. You may not remember me from--" He stopped me mid sentence, " I remember you young lady. Are you serious this time?" I didn't say a word. I simply handed him my test. Mr. Darnet flipped through the pages. He looked up with a slight smile on his face and said, "um hum." I felt pretty confident walking out of that room.

It took several weeks for me to get my score back. The results came in an official envelope in the mail. I couldn't get to its contents quick enough. My brother, Wayne, was there as I silently read and then exclaimed, "I passed! I PASSED BABY!" I was jumping and running around like a clown with the biggest smile on my face. Then I ran back towards him screaming, "Thanks Wayne! , Thank you, thank you so much," extending my arms to hug and kiss him. He pushed me back and asked, "What was your score?" I had to put a pause on my celebration to look for it. I looked at him, *What? Who the hell cares? I stopped reading at we are happy to inform you.*

I put a finger in the air signaling for him to wait a minute. Didn't he know I had only skimmed over the letter looking for keywords. Now I had to go back and actually read it. Here it is, needed score 70 out of 100, your score, 83! Yeah baby! It wasn't a 100, but it wasn't a 70 either. Wayne grunted his approval and went upstairs. I couldn't wait to tell my Mom. I told her the good news before she was in the house good.

I was called to the placement office to speak with a Counselor. Mrs. Carmichael was one of the few white faculty members on Campus. She was an older woman, with inviting soft blue eyes. She wore glasses, a lot of makeup, and painted her lips a bright red. She held several positions on campus. She was a Counselor in the Placement Center; she was my Department Head and my Advisor. She motioned for me to enter her office, smiled and said, "Have a seat Ms. Kershaw.Congratulations!" She seemed genuinely excited for me. Of course, it may have had something to do with the fact that I was the only student from Mills College to pass the FAA's test.

"Thank you." I took a seat in the first chair I got to. There was a folder on her desk with my name on it. She opened it as she started to talk.

"I called you here to schedule your interview with the FAA."

"Interview?" I instantly copped an attitude. "They never said anything about an interview. Why do I have to go on an interview? I've already passed the test. Are you saying I'm not hired? What, I don't have a job."

"Ms. Kershaw, calm down. I am not familiar with the hiring practices of the FAA. However, employers tend to interview potential employees." She paused looking at me over her glasses. "There will be a drug test as well."

"Did you say a drug test?" I needed verification. I wasn't sure I heard her correctly. Mrs. Carmichael said, "Yes, is there a problem?"

"No, not at all." I didn't hear anything else she said after drug test. I was too busy trying to figure out how to get my system clean. She gave me paper work with contact information on the person I needed to call and schedule the interview. I was nervous; I needed to talk to my girl and figure this out. I left her office nervous and scared as hell.

I called Maria and told her what Mrs. Carmichael told me. "Look Trish you've had a million job interviews. What's the big deal."

"The big deal is that I've never had a professional interview like this one! It's for the Government."

"Girl, just do a little blow and go with the flow."

"Are you crazy? I just told you they were going to do a drug test! Shit—I can't ever get high again!"

"Calm down, I was just kidding."

"I need to get clean. How do I get clean?"

"How long you got?"

"A few weeks."

Maria gave me her, "fail safe," plan on how to pass my drug test. Apparently, her brothers had taught her. Over the next few weeks, I was instructed to take three shots of apple cider vinegar, drink two gallons of water and a pitcher of some tea concoction daily. In addition to all the above, I was ordered to work out three times a day. If I didn't know any better, I would have sworn Maria was trying to kill me. Let's just say, I did what I could.

The interview was held at the Birmingham City Airport. They had what was called a Flight Service Station (FSS) at that time located on the grounds. I would later learn that there were three options available for an Air Traffic Control Specialist.

The first was The Flight Service Station option. Controllers, there worked closely and directly with the General Aviation (GA) Pilots. GA Pilots primarily flew small planes like, Cessnas, Pipers, or Citations. Most of those aircrafts were private owned by doctors, lawyers, controllers or whoever else had the money to buy one and pay for the flying lessons. Some GA Pilots were hired and flew for corporations. Most of your big companies such as: General Motors, Home Depot, Vanity Fair, and Mid First to name a few, owned private jets. Usually, those pilots were building their flight hours in an effort to get hired by the major air carriers. The FSS controllers provide those pilots with crucial weather information along their route of flight and assisted them with new routes if needed. They were also responsible for taking down important personal information from the pilots used for search and rescue in the event of an accident. Information such as: color of aircraft, contact numbers, and number of souls on board. All of this information was part of the pilot's flight plan. A flight plan, in simple terms, is your departure place and time, arrival place and time, and how you plan to get there. The FSS Controller entered the flight plan into the FAA's computer system and sent it to the controllers who would be providing service to the pilot.

The second was the Terminal or Approach Control Option, that's the one that most people are familiar with. Terminal Controllers worked in the Tower, (that tall building located on the airport grounds). The tower could be seen as you approached any airport. It had big glass windows all around it. By design, the height and windows gave the controllers an unobstructed panoramic view of the perimeter. Controllers in the tower needed to physically see the aircraft that were landing, departing as well as the ones taxiing or moving around on the grounds. That was upstairs. However, most people didn't know about the radar room downstairs at the base of those towers called the approach room. The controllers there would pick the aircraft up on radar and positively identify them. This was accomplished by assigning a 4 digit discrete number to the aircraft called a beacon code. They controlled a relatively small radius of airspace around the airport; usually between the altitudes of 10 and 14 thousand feet. The controllers downstairs would climb the aircraft to the top altitude of their stratum, radar identify them and hand them off to the third controller option.

The third and last option was the Air Route Traffic Control Center. There were 20 of these throughout the 48 contiguous states. The Center Controllers worked aircraft across large areas of airspace. For example, Atlanta Center's airspace covered parts of Georgia, Alabama, South Carolina, North Carolina, Tennessee, Kentucky,

West Virginia and Virginia. These controllers worked aircraft, in some areas, from the ground to infinity or as high as the aircraft could fly. The Center literally owned airspace up to flight level 999 into the Stratosphere. Center controllers, in my opinion, were the best of the best; cream of the crop and you had to know your stuff as you provided service to aircraft from state to state.

I scheduled the interview for a Tuesday. Tuesdays were my lightest days so it made sense. I drove my mom's car and parked where I had been instructed to do so. I entered the small gray brick building; greeted the secretary; signed my name on a list; was told to have a seat and Mr. Banks would be with me shortly. I wore a yellow two piece skirt set with a white blouse and black heels. I don't know where that outfit came from. Probably the Goodwill or Salvation Army. My sister-cousin got it for me. She was good with fashion and stuff like that. Although the fit was not perfect, it looked okay on me. It was the style of clothes she envisioned a person would wear on a professional job. It's funny how clothes can make you look older. That outfit aged me by at least 15 years.

A short white man with a receding hairline approached me and introduced himself as Mr. Samuel Banks. "We go by first names around here; feel free to call me Samuel." He was the Manager of the FSS. I stood, accepted his extended stubby hand with a firm grip and shook it as hard as I could. I had been told that showed confidence. I wanted to show him I was confident and I would be a good fit for the FAA. I introduced myself, "Hi I'm Patricia Kershaw, just call me — Patricia." For some reason Trish didn't seem befitting; it wasn't professional enough. I was no longer Trish; that naïve, gullible, pop eyed little girl that my family and friends knew. Over a short period of time, I had evolved into a serious scholar with goals, dreams and unforeseen opportunities. I was Patricia. And as I looked at the reflection of myself through the glass, I realized I was a good looking young woman; as beautiful as my sisters, in my own way.

He had me follow him into his office for the interview. It was the biggest office I had ever seen. It had a beautiful large mahogany desk with matching mahogany file cabinets that took up one half of the room and a conference table with six chairs around it occupying the other. He sat in an executive style high back burgundy leather chair and I sat in one of the two wingback burgundy leather chairs directly in front of his desk. The office walls were beige with bright abstract paintings hanging that added much needed color. Mixed in with the paintings were pictures of different airplanes, along with beautiful wood plaques, and gold framed certificates showcasing his many accomplishments. Pictures of his family members were strategically placed throughout the office. I was impressed, but I didn't want him to think I had never been in an office like this before, so I pretended this was normal. In reality, I wanted to tell him this was the baddest office I had ever seen and ask him who decorated it. After an endless stream of questions mixed in with frivolous conversation, the interview ended. Although I could not remember most of what was said during the interview, I left feeling good about my prospects.

Several weeks later, I received this letter from the FAA:

> Dear Ms. Kershaw:
>
> We are pleased that you have been selected to participate in our Cooperative Education Program. You will be given an accepted conditional appointment and be subject to the requirements of the Co-op Program agreement. Please note that this program does not guarantee permanent employment.

Your position will be Air Traffic Control Specialist, GS-2152-4, salary $12,862.

We would like for you to report for work at 8:00 a.m., September 3, 1985, to Mr. Carlisle Cook, Air Traffic Manager, Atlanta Air Route Traffic Control Center, 299 Woolsey Road, Hampton, Georgia. If you cannot report on this date or wish to decline this offer, please call me at (404) 763-7916.

If you have prior military service, please send copies of your DD-214's to the attention of ASO-12, immediately. It is necessary to verify your military services before your appointment is processed.

Your continued retention on this appointment will be contingent upon your meeting all other regulatory requirements after your entry on duty.

We welcome you to our Cooperative Education Program and look forward to a mutually rewarding experience.

Sincerely,

Greg W. Darnet

Personnel Staffing Specialist

Human Resource Management Division

I was selected for the F. A. A.'s Cooperative Education Program. It was a program designed to recruit minorities and women into the Administration. I later found out that I would work a semester and go to school a semester until I graduated. After which I would be sent to Oklahoma City to the F.A.A. Academy for further training. All of which was contingent upon me meeting requirements and successfully completing their program. After reading the letter, I ran into my mom's room to tell her the good news.

"Mom, I'm going to Atlanta Center to work! They're actually going to pay me twelve thousand dollars a year! Can you believe that?"

"Well, yes I can; I've always told you that you can do all things through Christ--". I cut her off "Yeah, yeah I know which strengthens me."

"Who strengthens me!" She immediately corrected with a hint of irritation in her voice.

"It says here that there will be 16 of us reporting. It has the names and numbers of everyone listed. It says we'll have to find a place to stay and we need our own transportation." I looked at mom who was looking at me with an, "Oh well," expression on her face. "Alrighty then, I'd better call some folks on this list to see who's staying where and who has a car."

The first person I called was Mr. Parks. He was our lead instructor. He had a raspy voice with the weirdest laugh I'd ever heard, but he seemed cool. I told him I was excited about the opportunity and about coming to Atlanta. I told him I needed a place to stay and that I did not have a car. He stated he would help me in any way possible and that he would have one of the other Co-Op students reach out. He had Jane to call me; she was from Memphis and a true one hundred percent southern belle. I didn't know they existed in the black race, but she was one, accent and all. She attended La More and Owens College an HBCU there in Memphis. She told me she was a Math Major. I was impressed and intimidated. Math majors were smart. We talked several times and hit it off immediately. We had a lot in common. We both came from large families and we were both determined to do great things. We just didn't know what yet.

Over the next few days, Mr. Parks found us a place to stay. He asked if we would be open to having two more roommates in order to save money. Jane and I agreed to the additional roommates. We both liked the sound of saving money. It turned out that none of us girls had cars. Mr. Parks suggested we ride with one of the male students in our class; so, he gave me Edward Jackson's phone number. Mr. Parks had found him a place not far from ours. I called Edward and we agreed on a price to be paid weekly for transportation to and from work. He made it clear that there would be additional charges for anything outside of work. Trips to the grocery store, laundromat, mall, and Church would be negotiated on an individual basis. He apparently had been a taxi guy on his campus. We all knew the racket because none of us had cars. We were well acquainted with the ride and pay system. With that taken care of, everything seemed to be falling in place.

It was hard to believe how much I had changed in just one short year. I had become more responsible. I had stopped doing drugs. And having a full plate or a load of things, in which everything had to be completed, taught me how to prioritize. I would soon find out that knowing how to prioritize was a key component to successfully becoming an air traffic controller. But, the most significant change came in the form of self awareness. I discovered I had an aptitude for study. All this time, I thought I was dumb. It turned out, I just needed to read more or shall I say read things more than once. Not everything, but the things that were difficult to me. I found myself reading them two or perhaps four times to fully grasp it. As a result, I studied longer and worked a little harder. I was becoming a Scholar. In my mind, I was the true definition of a scholar; one who had an aptitude for study.

CHAPTER SEVEN

THE JOURNEY BEGINS

Saturday August 31, 1985, the weekend before our first day at work, Jane and I arrived in Atlanta. Our other two roommates would arrive on Sunday. We wanted time to officially meet and greet each other without the interference of the other roommates. Our boyfriends would bring us and leave early Sunday morning before the other girls arrived. The plan was settled and just needed to be executed.

Approaching Atlanta from (I20) the city's skyline appeared like a beacon of hope. The tall buildings, shimmering from the sun's rays, stretching high towards the Heavens were a magnificent sight to see. They looked like mountains against the horizon. I likened it to how Dorothy must have felt as she laid eyes on the

Emerald City for the first time. Atlanta was my modern day Emerald City. A city where dreams came true and in it was my ticket to a new beginning, a fresh start, and another life.

Following the directions given to us by Mr. Parks, Reginald, (my boyfriend), and I exited I20 onto Lee Street. It was close to the HBCUs. The sidewalks were bustling with young black students that looked liked me. They were students with an attitude on a mission. They walked with a certain air about them; one of determination, pride, and purpose; but not arrogance. I loved everything about this area. It was called the West End. There were trendy shops, African Boutiques, and various eateries on the main strip. There were two drug stores, a Krispy Kreme doughnut shop, a steakhouse, and a MARTA Transit Station that helped make up this self contained Black community.

Our home away from home was four blocks away from the MARTA train station. This would come in handy down the road. We turned into the driveway and was stopped by a large wrought iron gate with pointed spikes on top of it. A light skinned bald black man, who looked to be in his 50s, opened the gate allowing us access onto the property. The driveway was paved with bricks and stones. As we slowly drove through the gates, I noticed that the entire lot was enclosed with this wrought iron gate that looked as if there were spears pointing out the top of it. There was a huge house that was the main quarters and a smaller one across the stoned driveway that was obviously used, once upon a time, as the servants' quarters. You could tell that back in the day this place was a magnificent estate, because it was still an awesome sight to see. This home took up an entire corner of a city block. Entering those gates was like going back in time. This quaint property was owned by Lawyer Baker. We came to know him as the slum lord. He owned property all over the West End area. The ones he rented to the Co-Op students were fully furnished and well kept.

Jane and I had planned the trip down to the last detail. We arrived within minutes of each other. At last, I finally met the girl who would be my roommate in Atlanta over the course of my Co-Op training. She was petite and I thought her voice matched her frame. She had flawless caramel colored skin and she wore a Jerry Curl that was shoulder length completing her entire look. She had on tight fitting blue jeans that accentuated her small frame. She was as cute as a button. We hit it off immediately.

"Patricia," she squeaked my name with a smile that displayed a set of perfect white teeth and dimples.

"Hey Jane," we extended our arms and greeted each other with a hug.

"This is Reginald my boyfriend."

In his deepest Barry White voice he said, "Hi Jane, nice to meet you; I've heard a lot about you."

"The pleasure is all mine. This is Al, my fiancé."

Oh, excuse me, she's engaged. Well, Reginald could be my fiancé if I wanted him to. Anyway, did I see a ring?

"Oh, congratulations."

We followed the guys' lead and greeted each of them with handshakes instead of hugs. Just as we were finishing up the introductions, Mr. Baker came over and took us inside what was to be our home away from home for the next three months. The smaller house had two bedrooms, one bath, a kitchen, a small dining area, and a living room. The entire house was completely furnished from the linen on the beds down to pots and pans in the kitchen. The only thing we had to bring was our clothes. Each room had twin beds with matching bedspreads. The house was furnished with second hand items probably bought from a yard sale. However, I didn't mind. It was the closest thing I had ever experienced to campus living and I was enjoying it all. After we took our bags in and started to unpack, we decided to get a bite to eat. We walked over and asked Mr. Baker if he knew a place close by where we could get some grub. He recommended a steak house right around the corner. Apparently, he must have forgotten we were poor, broke college students, because this place was way too expensive for us. Thank goodness our "working" boyfriends were there to pay for this meal. Otherwise, it would have taken every cent of my spending money for the month if I had to pay. Needless to say we didn't return there until after our second paycheck and it was only for drinks and appetizers.

The next day, our boyfriends left and the other two roommates arrived. I shared a room with Rhonda. Rhonda was the color of light brown sugar. She was full figured, solid, but not fat, in a stocky kind of firm way with bright twinkling eyes. She was good looking. Her hair looked as if she had just left the salon. She was well dressed, had lots of suitcases with the best smelling perfume I had ever smelled. This chick screamed money; however I'm not really sure if she had any. You know the type; the wannabe(s). They look the role, act the role, but lack the substance. She did nothing but complain the entire time she was there. Nothing was good enough for her. The house was too dusty; the bed was too small, the water was too hard, this wasn't right, that's all wrong, and so on and so on. I wanted to strangle her. After I got to know her; she turned out to be okay. She was just a little spoiled and on the wild side much like myself. I could handle that.

Jane shared a room with Rena. Rena was slightly darker than Rhonda. She was short and wore glasses with a crop haircut. She was more reserved like Jane. If you ask me; she seemed more on the sneaky side. You know the quiet sneaky ones that were smart in the classroom and freaky in the bedroom. She was average looking with a body to die for. It was the perfect match up. We all got along pretty good. However, Jane and I became very close. We would visit each other's home. She would take me sightseeing. We visited the home of Elvis Presley and the famous Beale Street. I would take her to nightclubs. Although we were as different as night and day, we still had a lot in common. She was cute. I was cute. She had six siblings. I had eight. She was reserved. I was wild. Hey, you know what they say opposites attract.

Next, it was time to meet the guys and our ride to work and our ride to anywhere else we needed to go. The two Ed(s) as I liked to call them. There was Eddie B. and Eddie J. They both had their own cars. Eddie B. was short, dark skinned with beady eyes. Eddie J. was tall, slim, brown complexion with slant eyes. They went to the same school and were the perfect roommates. We worked out a fee; which I thought was way too high, but what other choice did we have. They had the upper hand. They charged each of us twenty dollars a week for gas and extra if we needed a ride to the store or the laundromat.

"I have got to get me a car, Jane."

"Yeah, I need one also. Maybe, we can save up enough money to buy one."

"We'll have to if we don't want to continue to pay the Cassady boys the rest of our careers."

"Girl, you are silly."

"I know; but it makes life a little easier to deal with."

We needed groceries. The guys agreed to take us shopping. So we made our grocery list; Jane and Rena went shopping while Rhonda and I continued to unpack. We made it to bed around midnight, but I couldn't sleep. I was too excited about my new career. *I wonder what it will be like.*

Man, its two thirty in the morning. I need to get some sleep; the guys will be here at seven to pick us up.

It was September 3, 1985 . I'm not sure what time I went to sleep, but I knew six o'clock in the morning came way too soon. I managed to be ready when the guys arrived and we left for Atlanta Center at exactly seven. It took us 50 minutes to get there. We took interstate Seventy-five south for several miles. After which we had to exit to ride Georgia Highway Nineteen Forty-one for what seemed like an eternity. All the while I was thinking: *Where the hell are we? Are we lost? I'm not sure if they know this or not but we left Atlanta 30 miles ago. And this is not Hot-Lanta this is the boonies! Why the hell is this called Atlanta Center?*

The Center was actually located in a city called Hampton, Georgia; approximately 35 miles south of Atlanta. I would later find out that all of the centers were "strategically" located outside of the major cities in the event of war on our homefront. The powers that be thought it would be a good idea in the event of a major city bombing, that the National Air Traffic Service would go uninterrupted, (hopefully). Besides what country in their right mind would bomb a small country town like Hampton when Atlanta is that close; unless of course they're off target.

We pulled up to the gate to sign in and get passes into the building. The security guard phoned Mr. Parks and advised him that his students were here. He met us at the front door with the biggest smile you ever wanted to see. Mr. Parks was an average height, ebony complexion, weird looking brother with bloodshot red eyes. He looked as though he had been partying all night long. He escorted us to our room and we started as soon as all were accounted for. We had 16 students in our class. I later found out our class was the largest in the history of the center. We had four sisters, ten brothers, and two white guys in our class. I looked around the room at all the eager faces. *I thought this was a program to recruit minorities. I wonder what minority groups those two represented. Well, they are from Tennessee, perhaps the mountain people are a minority group or better still; they may be passing.*

Mr. Parks turned out to be our second in command. Our lead instructor was a fellow by the name of Don Mathis. He was an average height, pale white, slightly overweight guy with curly hair. He spoke with his teeth clenched and it got on my nerves. Thank goodness we didn't see him much.

The first day was filled with introductions and paperwork. I had to give an account of every job I had ever had. Do you know how painstaking that was? I think I must have had 18 jobs up until that point. The pressure was on, because I was told if I falsified the information I could lose my job. *Can they fire you before you start?* Anyway, I did the best I could. *Besides, isn't this Uncle Sam? Don't they know all?*

Over the next three months, I learned more about air traffic than I knew about my family's history. We studied the various types of aircrafts; followed by cloud types, formations and their impact on aviation; followed by area map readings and drawings; followed by phraseology; followed by proper strip marking and on and on. There was a tremendous amount of information to learn in a short period of time. I thought I was going to lose it. No parties for me. I had to hit the books every night. Let's face it, I wasn't the brain of the family. I was simply a scholar. Usually it was Jane and I at the house studying on the weekends while Rhonda, Rena, and the fellows hung out. After all, this was "Hot-Lanta" and we were college students. They wanted to see and do it all.

The semester had finally come to an end and I was glad to be leaving. I didn't have to work that hard in school. I was looking forward to the break. The hard work paid off for me. I was asked to return for phase two of the training. However, my roommate, Rhonda was not asked back.

It was time to go back to school. I had managed to save a little money and as soon as I returned home, I bought me a used car with the help of my Mom. She had an old gray Nova that was not running. She gave it to me to use as a trade in. I bought a Ford Fairmont. It was the same color as a lemon and believe me it was just that. I found another part- time job to help pay for my car, but I always needed money from Mom to help make ends meet. As usual, she would come through. Before I knew it; it was time to pack up and head back to Atlanta. However, this time I would have my own wheels.

Mr. Baker had rented our first place out to some guy. We were taken to another one of his houses several blocks away. The house was a white two-story duplex. We rented the downstairs and some guys rented the upper quarters. It was cozy; however, not as nice as the first house, nor did it seem as secure, but we managed to finish yet another semester. This one was not crammed with as much information. We spent time at each option of the F.A.A. learning how they interacted with the other. This also allowed us the opportunity to decide which option we preferred, Flight Service, Terminal, or En-route/Center. We opted for the Center option.

During our last weeks of training, we were taught how to run non-radar problems in the lab. We had new lab instructors; they were all retired controllers and all were white. There's one in particular I remember. His name was Red. He was an old, short, stocky, and very likable person. He just had one little-bitty problem. He couldn't keep his hands to himself. He liked, young black girls. With all of us young black college girls in and out of the lab, he probably thought he was at an all you can eat buffet. Of course, the term sexual harassment wasn't as prevalent back then.

As a matter of fact, I don't recall hearing about it until the late nineties; so we did the next best thing. We made a pact that went something like this:

"Jane, whatever you do; do not leave me alone in that lab with Red! He keeps rubbing my shoulders, then my back, and smiling at me with those stained yellow teeth asking: 'Do you understand precious?' *(I thought to myself yeah I understand; I understand I want you to quit touching me and brush your teeth).*"

"Gross! He's touching me to. Okay, it's a deal. We never leave each other alone with him."

So that solved our sexual harassment problem with Red. Too bad we didn't know about suing. We could have been set for life.

It was my senior year in college. I was taking over 20 hours my last semester in order to graduate in the spring of '87. I'm not sure exactly when or how it happened, but I was suddenly a confessed Atheist. I was simply too educated, (at this point in my life),to continue to accept the Bible's explanation of my existence. Besides there was no proof of the version, "And God Said Let There Be," it was based solely on someone's belief. The only thing that seemed logical to me for Man's being was Darwin's Theory of Evolution. Well, I didn't like the fact that I had come from an ape either, but I was educated now; all educated persons accepted this theory right?

In May, I graduated Magna Cum Laude. My Mom was there and most of my siblings. Even though Reginald and I had broken up at this point, he still managed to make my graduation. It was a great day and everyone I knew was happy and proud for me.

After graduation, I reported to Atlanta Center as a permanent, temporary employee of the F.A.A. That was in June of '87. The Atlanta Center's workforce at that time consisted of approximately 400 plus controllers. About 10 were black males and they had one black female who served as my role model. Her name was Joanne Hopkins. She was smart, educated, (that is she had a college degree unlike ninety five percent of the controller workforce at that time), and she had a sweet personality. I would be sitting in her seat before long. However, for the meanwhile I worked as an Air Traffic Controller Assistant from June until August of '87. It was a mindless useless job, but someone had to do it. You see, the controllers used computer printed flight plan information in conjunction with the radar to help them track the aircrafts. The computer printed information would have the aircraft's call sign, type, speed, altitude, route of flight, and other information on it. As an assistant, I was responsible for ripping the printout, (called a strip), off of the printer, placing it in a strip holder, and sitting it on the correct radar scope. It was easy to figure out which radarscope got which strip because each scope was numbered and the strips would have the numbered scope on it. I told you it was a silly job, but they had to do something with the persons in limbo like me as well as the washouts. Washouts were individuals that failed the training program. The Government finally got rid of the position, and the washouts; well, let's just say they try not to have as many.

The time had finally arrived for me to go to Oklahoma City, Oklahoma; home of the F.A.A. Academy. I was more than ready to show them what I was made of.

I would catch a flight to Memphis, hook up with my girl Jane, and we would be in OKC by three.

CHAPTER EIGHT

AIR TRAFFIC CONTROL: A RUDE AWAKENING

Jane and I flew into Oklahoma City, mid-August of '87. It was hot and windy.

"Alright Jane, you go and grab our bags, I'll look for the courtesy phones they told us about and call for our ride."

"Okay, just hurry back there's too many suitcases for me to carry by myself."

"Yeah from the looks of them all, you would think we were moving here permanently."

Jane went to look out for our luggage while I phoned the Rail Head for a ride. The Rail Head was the Apartment Complex that was to be our home for the next few months.

"Jane, they told me to look for a blue van and tell the driver to bring us to the Rail Head."

"Okay Patricia, look grab that one, that's the last piece."

"I think we better get a cart Jane."

"Behind you Patricia, over in the corner, get it fast before someone else gets it."

We pushed the cart outside. There were at least five blue vans parked in a row. "How lucky." There was a guy standing in front of one of the vans. He asked, "Where to ladies?" "The Rail Head, please." The ride to the Rail Head only took ten minutes. However, I still remember thinking how everything looked so flat and long. There weren't a lot of trees and the ones that I saw all seem to lean in the same direction; probably from the constant wind pushing them that never stopped blowing. The Rail Head was an F.A.A. only apartment complex. They rented one, two, and three bedroom apartments to students attending the Academy. Business, for places like this in the city, had been lucrative since the Controller strike of '81. We were paid our salary plus given a per diem to cover our housing and food while here. Apparently, the Rail Head knew exactly what we received because that's what they charged to the penny. We checked in and were shown to our apartment. It was on the second floor. We had two bedrooms, two baths, a living room, kitchen, and a dining room. It was perfect. There was a desk, a map of the airspace we would be learning, as well as a non radar board (that was two pieces of plywood attached together at an angle with slates that we used to place pieces of paper with flight plan information on it called strips), strip holders, and controller pencils. They really catered to the F.A.A. students.

"Jane I can't believe this hook up? They have thought of everything; right down to the ruler and paper to draw our maps with."

"Well, I guess that's what we're paying the big bucks for. They have a pool and the receptionist said that tonight is free pizza and beer night at the guest house."

"Look Jane, for the money they're charging the government it ought to be free night every night." Jane laughed." Girl, you're crazy, but I think they may have something here at least three nights out of the week."

"Get out of here."

Well, Jane was right they had Italian night, Mexican night, Chinese night, and only God knows what other kind of night with all the free beer you could drink. We were having fun and living large.

The Academy on the other hand was the complete opposite. It was all work there and no play. It looked like a college campus. There were several buildings that made up the complex. As we approached the campus heading south on

MacArthur street, to the west stood a unique gray modern building. I would later learn that it was indeed one of the newest buildings. It was called the Stafford Building, and it housed the terminal radar lab. It was an impressive piece of architecture named for an astronaut. There were two buildings on the east side of MacArthur. One was the Academy Building and the other was named the Air Traffic building. I would later spend most of my time in the Air Traffic building. That was where my phase of the air traffic training was conducted. Further south on the east side stood a large square shape building that reminded one of an elementary school. This building had tall flag poles in front of it. It was the Headquarters building. We had our first all hands assembly there. It was also the place were they conducted the graduation ceremonies for new Air Traffic Controllers. Although most of the buildings were old, they were all clean and well kept. Most of the landscaping consisted of leaning trees and shrubs. I don't recall much color anywhere, not even inside the buildings. It felt cold. The place was very regimented.

Our first day consisted of checking in, more paperwork, taking pictures for identification cards and newspaper articles (in the event you graduated) and briefings on what to expect while in training at the Academy. We were sent to the Headquarters Building for an assembly in the main auditorium. We were given a welcome speech, that is I thought it was a welcome speech until I heard the man say," I want each of you to look to your left, now look to your right. One of those persons will not make it through this program. We have a 60% washout rate."

And he said those words as if he was proud of the fact that tax payers were paying millions of dollars to bring us out here, just to have him wash us out or fire us. I sat there thinking what a jerk and oh thanks for the vote of confidence. *I'm sure we'll do just fine without your support.*

He ended his speech by saying, "Less than half of you will complete this program successfully. That half will be sent to the field, (Terminals and Center), and out of those numbers only half will actually make it to become a Full Performance Level Controller."

"Oh isn't that great news Jane why even bother? He should just have us count off now and send the odd numbers back home."

"Shhh be quiet we need to hear this."

"I don't need to hear this depressing crap. This is an outrage. I didn't bust my butt studying all those late nights and weekends in Atlanta for this clown to tell me I'm not going to make it. I'm not accepting this bull; he can go jump off a bridge."

The next several weeks consisted of drawing maps, learning non radar separation rules, Standard Operating Procedures (SOPs) as well as Letters of Agreements (LOAs) for a make believe facility called Aero Center. The separation rules,

LOAs and SOPs were what we applied to move aircraft in and out of Aero Center. Basically, these were agreements made between facilities that were adjacent to you; your next door neighbors. You needed to understand how to apply all the rules, SOPs, LOAs and you needed to know your airspace like you knew your neighborhood in order to be successful. So we drew and redrew every airway, jet airway, intersection, airport, special use area, and mileage distance between two points. Next, the class learned the rules used to keep aircraft separated in a non radar environment. The ten minute, twenty minute, fly back and miles divergence rules. We drilled each other and practiced everyday. Although most of this stuff was a review for Jane and I, we still couldn't afford to take it lightly. We, unlike Atlanta Center's previous Co-Op classes, had been trained well by the facility and needed to prove ourselves. Mainly because up until our class of sixteen students; Co-Op Students from

Atlanta Center had experienced a high failure rate at the Academy. As a matter of fact, I think only one Co-Op student from Atlanta Center had ever passed. This was through no fault of their own. We later found out the Atlanta Center Training Department had not been properly training their Co-Op Students. Somehow the "white" powers that be, at Atlanta Center thought the "mostly black" Co-Op students (i.e. interns) hired by the FAA to be trained as Air Traffic Controllers were getting an unfair advantage. Apparently, the Training Department did not want to give the students an unfair advantage. Racism will cause you to do backwards crazy things; like wasting taxpayers money. Up until our class, Atlanta Center's Training Department had blown thousands of the FAA's dollars on the unfortunate students that preceded us. It was an awful shameful act and waste of talent as well as funds.

After about a month and a half of classroom training which consisted of rotating days and evening shifts, it was time for the practice non-radar problems. The non-radar problems were ran in a lab. You would have one student controller being graded and another pretending to be the pilots as well as other controllers from the different facilities/options/neighbors, (that student was called the remote). The remote had the hardest job, but the pressure was on the graded student to pass. The object of the problem was to move the planes from point A to point B without running them into each other and without violating, or in other words trespassing, on/in another facility's airspace. This is when it all came together. The remote would call you, "AERO CENTER this is N1234P at Ponca City requesting clearance to Tulsa." The clock started, your hands would start to sweat, your stomach would turn as your throat became dry and squeaky. You had to visualize in your mind first, where the airport was located. Then, who owned the airspace, was there a facility to coordinate with prior to departure, what rule do I use to get him airborne and most importantly, what other traffic (and there was always other traffic) do I have to keep him separated from. Oh, did I mention that these problems were timed and you were expected to get all your departures off of the ground? It was a nightmare. I had never experienced anything like it in my life. I liken it to the equivalency of obtaining a four year degree in four months. The word stressful does not explain what I experienced. I was on an emotional roller coaster. On the days I passed a problem, I would feel great. I was walking on cloud nine. Then, the next day I would fail. I would call back to the Atlanta Center Training Department in a state of hysteria sobbing uncontrollably.

"What the heck is a fly back? You didn't teach us anything about a fly back. I failed this problem. I think Jane did also."

The unfortunate instructor who answered the phone would always reassure me that all was well.

"Calm down. It's going to be fine. These are only the practice problems. This is where you want to make your mistakes, get corrected, and perform well on your graded problems. Got it?"

"Yeah, you're right, but" he quickly interrupted me.

"I know, that's one we need to include in the training. Thanks for bringing it to our attention. Relax, you've got this."

Things were getting out of control fast. Jane my partner for the last two years had suddenly realized that this was not for her. *Oh great, not now Jane, we've come too far.*

"What do you mean? You don't think you were cut out to be a controller? Of course you were; we both were. This is crazy."

"Look Patricia, I've given this some serious thought. I didn't just wake up this morning and say hey, I don't think I want to do this anymore. This was a hard decision for me. I've prayed about it and I know that this is the right move for me. I plan to continue to work for the F.A.A. I've already spoken with Management back at Atlanta Center. They contacted the Manager at Memphis Center and I'll be working there as an Air Traffic Controller Assistant."

"You've got to be kidding. That is a dead end job! You are way too talented and far too smart for that."

"Yeah I know, but it's just until I can find something else in the F.A.A. that better suits my personality."

"I don't understand Jane, why didn't you tell me before now? Apparently there's nothing I can say to change your mind. Well, at least you've done your homework—

what can I say? You know I don't want you to leave. — Jane, I'm not sure if I can do this without you."

"Listen Patricia, you can do anything you put your mind to. You've always been the one pushing and prodding both of us. You were the one determined and destined for this career. Believe me, you will make it — and without me."

"So when are you leaving?'

"Tomorrow; Al and I are getting married soon and he's coming to get me."

"Wow, that's fast. I guess it's just me now. I'll see you in the morning."

That night I cried for three hours. What was I going to do now? Who could I count on, or talk to when I needed someone? Who would be there to encourage me?

I called my Mom and she told me that everything would be alright. "Baby, just pray and ask God for His help and guidance. He didn't bring you this far to leave you. We can do all things through Christ who strengthens us."

"Yes Momma, okay thanks. I love you."

"I love you too."

Just pray!? Just pray she says, but I'm an Atheist. Hasn't she listened to anything I've said since my senior year of college!? As the tears started a new steady stream down my cheeks I found myself on my knees kneeling beside the bed. Still too stubborn to call on the name of Jesus I cried out: "Superior Being whoever you are, whatever you are. I need your help. I need someone, somebody, or something stronger than me to lean on! I need help! I'm tired. I'm stressed. I'm scared. If you get me through this, I promise I will never deny you again."

You know, God is so merciful. In spite of my arrogance, in spite of my ignorance, in spite of my total disrespect for my upbringing, God showed up and intervened. Not on my behalf, but on the covenant he had with my Mother. The prayers of the righteous availeth much. I had a praying Mother.

There was a peace that fell on me like none other I had ever experienced. I slept soundly that night.

CHAPTER NINE

YOU CAN DEPEND ON GOD AND ONLY GOD

It was Saturday morning October 27, 1987. I heard voices up front. I stumbled to my feet and went straight to the living room without brushing my teeth. As I suspected; it was Al and Jane. She was all packed and ready to go.

"Hey sleepyhead, did we wake you?"

I lied, "No, no I was up. I wanted to wait until you were finished packing before I came out. So you finished packing?"

"Oh. Yeah; we're all set and ready to go." We stared at each other awkwardly. Not really knowing what to say. Finally Jane said: "You know I think that girl from Chicago what's her name?"

"Who do you mean Christine?"

"Yeah— she's the one."

"What about her?"

"I think you two would be perfect roommates. She still lives alone. You should ask her if she is interested in being your roommate. That way you'll have someone to study with."

"Well... I'm not sure."

"What do you mean you're not sure? You two would be great together. You both have outgoing personalities, you both like to party and you both smoke. You couldn't ask for a better person."

"You got a point there. I think I'll talk to her about it tomorrow. Although, I really don't party that much anymore; who has the time?"

"Just do it, don't think about it.— We'd better get on the road. Hey— stay in touch. Just because I'm not physically here doesn't mean I can't be here for you when you need me in spirit." We reached out and embraced each other. "I love you and I'll miss you. Knock them dead."

I held her tight not wanting to let her go. "I love you to. You've been like a sister to me. Take care and I'll see on the flip side."

I stood outside on that cold windy October morning for what seemed like an eternity. Willing her to stop and change her mind. She never did.

The next day I went over to visit with Christine. We talked and laughed for hours. I told her that Jane had left and she felt genuinely bad about it.

"Girl— Jane should have recycled."

"Recycled what's that?"

"It's what you do when you need to start over around here. Everyone does it."

"What are you talking about Christine?"

"I've recycled. You just go to CAMI to see the Doctor, tell him or her that you're sick and have some type of problem that won't allow you to focus, and he or she writes you a letter dismissing you from the training." I later found out that CAMI stood for The Civil Aviation Aero Medical Institute. They had an office staffed with doctors on campus.

"What do you mean dismissing? I don't know about that one Christine. It sounds so—so permanent."

"Look girl, it's not like you're fired. Think about it. As an Air Traffic Controller, you must be at your best 100% of the time. You have to have total concentration. They don't want us doing this job half here; not even in training. I heard that once a student flipped out and went insane out here in this program."

"Get out of here. Are you serious? What happened?"

"Well I wasn't here, but this is what I heard. He was getting ready for the graded non radar problems when it all overwhelmed him. They say he tried to hijack a plane over at Will Rogers Airport to take him home."

"No way!"

"Yes way."

"So think about it. The Government doesn't want to take a chance like that. They would be liable. So that's what students do around here when they're undecided or simply about to wash out; they go to CAMI for a second chance. They get recycled. Girl, I was flunking out. I just needed a little more time than they allowed us to grasp this stuff. So I got a medical excuse to be recycled. Got it?'

"Yeah I guess so, but it's too late for Jane now. Besides, she already knows she doesn't want to control airplanes for the rest of her career."

"Oh well. — So you're living by yourself now, right?"

"Yes as a matter of fact I am and that's part of the reason I came to see you. Would you be interested in having a roommate?"

"Sure Patricia that would be cool, but under one circumstance."

"What's that?"

"We move out of the Rail Head. I'm sick of the bus."

"I hear you, so am I. It would be nice to rent a car, but we can't afford that."

"We don't have to. I met some guys who rent from a man for just a little more than we pay, and he throws in a car."

"Really? Are you sure? That doesn't sound legit."

"Yes really and it's legal! The places are completely furnished with a washing machine and dryer and they are super nice."

"Okay, fine with me. When do we move out?"

"Tomorrow."

"Tomorrow? What about the money I've already paid to the Rail Head?"

"They'll just have to reimburse you for the amount of time you're not occupying the property. Listen, I'm on an evening shift. I'll take care of everything. All you have to do is pack."

"Okay Christine, if you say so. I'll see you tomorrow."

Christine was right this guy had the hook up. Mr. Green was his name. Mr Green was a short brown brother with a receding hairline. He owned homes and duplexes all over the Southside of Oklahoma City. Not only did he have rental property, but he also had a car rental place. He rented them out to F.A.A. students and made a killing.

This place was beautiful. It had an atrium with trees and plants growing inside in the foyer right as you walked in. It was a little more expensive because of it, but Christine said we needed to relax after a stressful day of training. And, as ridiculous as it sounded I was inclined to agree with her.

The graded problems were starting soon and the practice problems were beginning to get tougher. I was flunking most of them and the ones I did pass, I barely passed. I had to get serious. Drastic times called for drastic measures.

Christine would play a lot of contemporary Gospel music and she liked going to Church. I particularly liked this female group she played called The Clark Sisters. They had a nice beat and the sisters could blow. I would find myself singing along with them around the duplex, "Angels watching over me." I wanted desperately to believe that. I even started going to Church with Christine. It was a small Apostolic Church on the East side of town. It reminded me of the one I grew up in. For the first time in months I felt good. I felt confident in my ability to accomplish what I came out to the Academy to do. All I needed was a plan of action.

We formed study groups. Anyone who wanted to join in could. We would meet over to each other's place, set up our equipment, run problems until we got tired or passed out from the alcohol. Whichever came first.

I was getting good at the practice problems. I was so engrossed in them I found myself able to recall every call sign, altitude, route of flight, and request of all the aircraft involved in the problem. I would rush home from class, reconstruct the problem and run it with my study group the next day. When it was time for the graded problems; I was ready.

It was the Friday before the graded problems were to begin. Students had planned to have parties all weekend with the anticipation of not being able to party as much after the graded problems started. The Instructors told us to get a lot of rest over the weekend and try not to party the entire time. We were also told to look the part of a controller. Dress in a professional manner and look confident. I took every word to heart. I only went out Friday night. I studied all day Saturday and picked up again Sunday after Church.

Its funny how when things are going fine and everything is great we never think about God, but the moment the tide turns. I hate to admit that I was one of those persons who only called on God when I needed Him; however, at the same time I was glad I had enough sense to call on Him period.

CHAPTER TEN

ONE PHASE DOWN: FOUR MORE TO GO

The day of our first graded problem had finally arrived. Students came dressed in their Sunday best; all looking the part of young professionals. The guys had on shirts with ties and some even wore suits. The ladies had on pretty dresses, stockings and high heeled shoes. I had on a cute two piece beige skirt set with a pair of black pumps. My hair was down; It had been cut into an asymmetrical bob. I thought I looked fly, slightly conservative and somewhat sexy. It was the 80s, what can I say. I tried to eat something, but I couldn't. My stomach was in knots. You could sense the uneasiness in the air. The tension was so thick you could slice it with a knife. My class would be the first to start. In a way that was comforting. I would have it over with the first part of the morning, and if all went well; I would be able to eat lunch. I was weak and I was starving.

It was 8:30, time to go into the lab. We formed a line outside of the entrance and waited until the instructors told us to come in. Once given the go ahead to enter; we proceeded to do what we had practiced over the last few weeks. I was running first; which meant I was first up in the hot chair to be graded. My lab partner was the remote. The remote played the part of the pilot and neighboring facilities. I only had ten minutes to setup and pre-plan my moves. I sat down, put on my headset and commenced to stuffing the flight plan progress strips as fast as possible.

My next step was to look for traffic and possible solutions. If you had two aircraft at the same altitude within ten minutes of each other, that was a conflict or an issue that needed to be resolved. We were taught to write in red a different altitude, in which we would request the aircraft moved to in an effort to get him out of harm's way. The key was not to put him in conflict with another aircraft along his route of flight. You also had aircraft that were arriving into different airports. They needed to get underneath all crossing traffic safely and not hit any departing traffic from that airport. This took up a lot of my time. I looked at the preplan clock. I had three minutes left. The last thing I planned for were the departures. I quickly looked at their proposed departure times to see if any two aircraft had departure times that were within five minutes of each other off of the same airport. If so, I had to apply a non radar departure rule to safely get them airborne without any delays. Of course they all were. I looked at the types and filed airspeeds to determine which nonradar rule to use on the successive departures. I looked at their route of flight to see, what airborne traffic I had to miss and with whom I needed to coordinate. I needed to get them off the ground and airborne safely. I managed to pre-plan departure clearances for two of the four departures in my suspense bay before the time was up and the Lead Instructor stopped us. I just prayed that they were right.

The Lead Instructor announced loudly, "Time!" That was the shortest ten minutes of my life. Everybody stopped writing in mid stroke and we put down our controller pens. This was done in an overly exaggerated move by all of us, because no one wanted to risk failing for something as simple as not following the rules. You see; the Government was a stickler for rules. I rubbed my hands together thinking: if only I had a little more time. I needed a little more time. However, that was not possible. The rules stated you only got 10 minutes to pre-plan. You could literally hear the heartbeats in the lab. It would soon be time to start the problem. My entire career, my livelihood, my future, all that I had worked so hard for these past two years; would be determined at the end of the next 30 minutes. Then I heard those two words out of the Lead Instructor's mouth that propelled me into another world, "Clock's on." That meant it was time to start. We picked up our controller pens; it was game time baby. Suddenly, an explosion of voices, from 24 students with different dialects, sounded and engulfed the room speaking a new language we had learned called phraseology. With this learned phraseology we issued clearances talking fast and furious:

"D1 – D2"

"D1 – "

"Reference N1234P at Fort Smith (FSM)."

"Go ahead."

"Request N1234P at six thousand for traffic" (then you would sign off using your initials)

"VP"

"Show it Mike Zulu" (some students would use the phonetic spelling when giving their initials)

"Memphis Center Aero Center"

"Memphis Center go ahead"

"At Fort Smith N8546P request the aircraft at eight thousand right altitude for direction of flight VP"

"MZ"

(Now for the Aircrafts on frequency)

"AAL349 maintain one five thousand until four niner miles northeast of Ponca City cross one five miles northeast of Ponca City at and maintain six thousand Tulsa altimeter two niner niner two."

"AAL349 WILCO" (WILCO was approved phraseology for will comply)

The explosion in the room got my adrenaline pumping and my hands were sweating. I heard voices cracking; it was both exciting and terrifying. While all of this was going on, I was cognizant of the Instructor seated behind me who appeared to be constantly writing. Every time he would scribble I thought the worst and wanted to second guess myself. But the clock was on; there was no going back. I had to believe God or a, "superior being" had my back and I was prepared.

Although the problem only lasted 30 minutes, it seemed liked three hours. I heard the instructor say, "Okay I've seen enough. Good job." I looked at the clock; only 28 minutes and 40 seconds had passed. I felt good, but he stopped the problem before the 30 minutes were up. A million thoughts ran through my mind: *Did I mess up in the last few minutes? He stopped the problem early, but he said I did a good job. What's going on. Looking over my strips, I didn't see any separation errors that would immediately fail me.* Usually, stopping the problem early would be an indication that I had failed it. With wet rings under my arms from the perspiration, a dry mouth from all the talking and a feeling of total vulnerability, I waited for the debriefing as he wrote his final comments. The instructors always made a point to tell you the good before the bad. I think they must have been trained that way, because they all did it. It was like the calm before the storm. You know what I mean, you did well but bam.

After he finished writing, he examined my flight plan progress strips looking for any incorrect strip markings to add to his write up. If you had any, he would bring it to your attention and take off points from your grade. I worked hard and practiced daily on strip marking in order to perfect it. Those were precious points, I could not afford to give up. I had no errors. Next on his list was phraseology. Phraseology, much like strip marking, was simple route memory training. The things you learned, used daily and would be foolish to lose a single point on. So I made it my business to learn to read, write and speak my new language. And I was fluent in it. Needless to say, I did not have any phraseology erros. The Instructor was impressed. Next he proceeded to show me alternate ways on how to get the same job done. I took notes, this would serve me well on the next graded problems. Again he was impressed that I was taking notes and asking questions during the debrief. Although he showed me different ways to move the aircraft from point A to point B easier, he did not mention me running two of them together and he had not stopped the problem too early. Once again, it was well known, if you had any separation errors, (running two planes together), on a graded problem, you automatically failed. The clock was stopped. You were washed out of the program. You were sent back to your home facility for placement. That is, if they could find you something. Normally there was always something for the ones they liked. Even if it was the mindless Air Traffic Assistant Position of ripping strips. It was time for him to tally up my score. You needed a 70 or higher to pass. I made a

93. He had taken off points for not getting all the departures off. That was considered delaying the aircraft. I was elated. I could not contain myself. I went running and jumping out of that lab like a kid on Christmas morning.

So it continued like that for the next week and a half. I averaged an 85 or higher on all of my graded problems. Although I did not finish with the highest score in my class, I was in the top five percent.

Out of my original class of 16 Cooperative Educational students, six of us successfully completed the program and were assigned to field facilities.

The two Ed(s) successfully completed the Non Radar Screen at the Academy. However, one quit the Administration and went to work for a private company. The other was assigned to Jacksonville Center.

I was the only female out of my co-op class to successfully complete the Non Radar Screen at the Academy. One was washed out of the co-op program early on while still in college. One went to the Academy two classes ahead of Jane and I; she washed out of the program there. Jane as you know resigned from the Air Traffic Option and is presently working For the F.A.A. at one of the Centers in Automation.

My new roomate, Christine, never completed the Academy. However, she now works for the F.A.A. as an aircraft mechanic.

In the winter of '87 and after nearly two years, I had officially become an F.A.A. employee. Successfully passing the Academy made me a federal employee with all their rights and privileges. I returned to Atlanta Center to start another phase of training, which was to include additional classroom training, as well as on the job training. Atlanta Center and Georgia was now my new home.

I returned home a hero. Our class had proven that ZTL's Co-Operative Education program could be a success. However, for me the real work was about to begin. And based on what I had just been through; I knew the next two and a half years of training would not be easy. My road to Full Performance Level Controller Journeyman was really just starting. I would have to dig deep, work hard and develop a closer relationship with God in order to pull it off.

Looking back, I have no regrets. However, if given a second chance I would certainly do some things differently. The Bible says the prayers of the righteous availeth much, and I had a praying Mother. Thankfully for me, by the time I had entered young adulthood, she had become a Prayer Warrior. She had been on the battlefield in a spiritual warfare for decades in the fight of her life. She was warring for her family. To the Devil, she had become a force to be reckoned with and one that would not quit.

When I got on a different path; I started to make better decisions. I felt in control as I soared through Mills college and the FAA's Co-Op program On a Wing and a Prayer. However, Controlling It in the ATL would be another story.

EXCERPT FROM CONTROLLING IT IN THE ATL:

I walked into the classroom. It was much smaller than the conference room that had been used for my Co-Op classes. There were eight four by four tables arranged in the small space. Each space had paperwork, books, a controller pen, an ink pen, a marker and a blank name tag. You sat where you wanted. Being there were only eight students or shall I say, FAA Employees assigned for training, I sat at one of the two tables in the front of the class. The class make up was what I would become to know as the norm in the 80s FAA. There was myself, the only black female; one black male, one white female and five white males. Our lead instructor came in followed by four other old white men, (presumably instructors), and he was the only familiar face in the crowd. What was happening? Did I not just spend two years as a Co-Op here in this facility? Where were the instructors I had come to know and depend on? Who were these old men? I later found out that each phase of training had its own group of instructors. Perhaps I didn't know as much as I thought. Something told me I was in for more late nights of studying and nothing was going to be easy.......

Patricia is faced with more obstacles and even bigger stumbling blocks on her journey to becoming an Air Traffic Controller in Atlanta Center. In the sequel: Controlling It in the ATL, she will have to tackle sexual harassment and discrimination in the workplace all while struggling with her biggest demon yet; her sexuality. In this book, we will experience Patricia's transition into womanhood and her path to making history in Atlanta Center.

ABOUT THE AUTHOR

Priscilla Russell is a wife, mother, grandmother, sister, aunt and most importantly a child of God. She loves to travel and spend time with family. At 55 years of age, Priscilla is a recently retired Air Traffic Controller who worked for the Federal Aviation Administration (FAA) over 32 years. She has worked Radar Positions at the busiest Air Route Traffic Control Center (ARTCC) in the world, Atlanta ARTCC in Hampton, Ga. She was the first African American female in the history of Atlanta ARTCC to be selected as a Front-Line Manager (FLM) in 1994. Priscilla has worked in various FAA Staff Positions and she was an FAA Academy Instructor. She has a Master of Science Degree in Space and Aviation Technology from Oklahoma State University and a Bachelor of Arts Degree in Communications from Miles College in Fairfield, Alabama. She used the two degrees and set out on this new path. Priscilla prays that this journey will be as rewarding and fulfilling as her last.